SOMETIMES I LIVE IN THE COUNTRY

OTHER BOOKS BY FREDERICK BUSCH

I Wanted a Year Without Fall
Breathing Trouble
Manual Labor
Domestic Particulars
The Mutual Friend
Hardwater Country
Rounds
Take This Man
Invisible Mending
Too Late American Boyhood Blues

SOMETIMES I LIVE
IN THE COUNTRY

Frederick Busch

DAVID R. GODINE • PUBLISHER • BOSTON

First published in 1986 by
David R. Godine, Publisher, Inc.
Horticultural Hall
300 Massachusetts Avenue
Boston, Massachusetts 02115

The lyrics found on page 75 are from "Goodnight Irene,"
words and music by Huddie Ledbetter and John A. Lomax.
TRO—© Copyright 1936 (renewed 1964) and 1950 (renewed
1978) Ludlow Music, Inc., New York, N.Y. Used by
permission.

LIBRARY OF CONGRESS CATALOGING IN PUBLICATION DATA

Busch, Frederick, 1941–
    Sometimes I live in the country.

    I. Title.
PS3552.U814S66   1986   813'.54   85-45975
ISBN 0-87923-622-1

Set in Caledonia by Graphic Composition, Inc., Athens, Georgia
Printed and bound by Haddon Craftsmen, Scranton, Pennsylvania
Designed by Dede Cummings

First edition
PRINTED IN THE UNITED STATES OF AMERICA

*To Helen Burroughs
and to the memory of
Allan H. Burroughs*

※　※　※

THE SKY SAT on top of their hill. He was in between the grass and the black air and the stars. Pop's
gun was black too and it was colder than the ground.
It filled his mouth. It was a small barrel but it filled
his mouth up. He gagged on the gun that stuffed his
tongue up into his head. He decided to close his eyes.
Then he opened them. He didn't want to miss anything. He pulled the trigger but nothing happened.
He didn't want to pull the trigger but he did. He
closed his eyes and that made it easier. He tightened
on the trigger and the sight came up onto the roof of
his mouth and he heard the click inside his head. Then
he took the revolver out of his mouth and wiped it on
his shirt. He put the safety back on and went down
the hill across from their house. He climbed the tilted
barbed-wire fence and crossed the road and went inside. In the kitchen he wrapped the pistol in its gray

3

felt cloth that said Oneida Cutlery and he set it back in the roasting pot on the bottom shelf of their pantry. He poured himself a glass of milk and he washed the glass. He went to bed.

In the morning Petey smelled his pop's after-shave that smelled like fags in the subway. He thought about telling Miz Bean something about subways. She would know about them except how they smelled in the rush hour when the creeps were there wearing Pop's after-shave and letting their hands fall onto your balls like an accident. Up here you smelled horses and cows and the only fag smell was his father. He wasn't a fag. He was a tough-ass who wore tight shirts and had uncool sideburns and a heavy neck. His belly hung right in there too. He could lift you up in the air and shake you when he lost his temper. He had done that once or twice.

When they drove in Petey looked straight ahead into the dust of their road. They went past the trailers and the shitshacks. People up on their road lived in trailers with tents pitched next door because they had so many kids and no money. They built little log cabin shitboxes onto the trailers and one of them kept this tin roof on with old tires because of the wind. Pop had bought the white house and all the land around them and the pond. They lived with all these creeps around them in trailers and shitboxes just out of sight. It was embarrassing to have a house that big around here. Down in the town after they had gotten onto the paved part of the road they passed where a guy sold purple hearts and bombers and of course what he told the cornheads was good grass. Petey was pretty sure it was mostly straw with a little grass plus maybe

4

oregano and cowpiss mixed in or something. He looked away.

Pop said, "I know about it."

"Huh?"

"I already know about it. The green house with the barn next to the lawn. I don't bust guys anymore."

"What, Pop?"

"Anyway, you don't touch that stuff, do you? That's the only reason I'd do those characters now. If they were putting something into your body that could hurt you."

Petey nodded and didn't look at Pop. He felt himself blushing.

The parking lot was huge and the school was huge. About fifteen school buses were dumping all kinds of farmers and bimbos and small smelly people into the central school. Petey got out of the car to go in. His father called, "Have a good day."

Petey waved behind him.

His father said with a different voice, "Take it easy." Except it said: Watch Your Ass.

Petey stopped and turned around because that voice told him to. He waved again except this time he looked at Pop and Pop waved back. That was all right and everybody showed their manners and he walked into the middle of the bimbos and cornheads.

Later on he saw Miz Bean talking to Pop near the cafeteria. She was tall but Pop was taller. But she was tall and she had big shoulders. She had a long nose. She wasn't like a model on TV. Which Pop made him turn off a lot because turning off the TV would make him get all As and stop ruining his chances for college at thirteen. Pop had this problem with college. Miz

Bean was having a good time with Pop. He looked like a guy in Queens they once visited. He was a retired cop who owned a bar near the airport. Pop was talking with the guy about the guy's wife. The guy was crying. Pop looked lousy. Pop looked a little bit like him except his hair was longer and a little white where the uncool sideburns started the big trip down next to Pop's long ears. Pop looked like a retired Irish cop. Petey laughed at that one and DiStefano said, "What's it taste like, man?"

Petey said, "Your sister."

DiStefano looked like he was deciding whether he should die for his sister's honor or just try and cripple Petey. Petey felt his face sneer. That was the word that went with what his father's face also did sometimes. It bent down all over except for the nose. That opened wide and he looked like he just stepped in dogshit on a hot day on Flatbush Avenue. DiStefano decided not to defend his sister's name.

"Good idea," Petey said. "Seeing that you don't have any sisters. Remember, stupid?"

"What?"

"But your *mother*," Petey said.

Pop heard their feet squeak in their sneakers on the green floor while they wrestled around. He turned. Petey had been keeping his eye on Pop. He pointed at Petey and Petey stopped. Pop went back to talking with Miz Bean. Petey went to class. DiStefano skipped to keep up with him. DiStefano was always trying to keep up. Pop stayed there. He was the guidance person in charge of attendance and assholes who came in late and the sneak-smokers and whoever carried knives in for fighting. Miz Bean stayed there too. She was the head guidance counselor and the one you had to talk to about your life.

They did Calhoun. He was the Great Compromiser, Miz Carver told them. She had a body like *Penthouse*. They changed at the bell and spent the next two class modules with Mr. Bell. He told them what they needed to know about getting diseases from sex. Petey kept his head down when everybody was laughing but he listened. He wanted to know precisely how you got the diseases. Nobody told them where to put what. He was pretty sure. But you didn't want to start in on something like that unless you had it right. He had heard there were a lot of places to get lost down there. Then the mods were over and they changed for lunch. Here was everybody's chance to show how totally repulsive they were. Petey cut out after the spit wads got sickening. It worked out that he was near Miz Bean's office. He could see her feet. She had long feet and long legs and they were sticking into the doorway. She was slumped down and he thought she was asleep. She had a paper bag over her head. Everybody's name was on the light green sofa. She wanted everybody to sign her sofa, she had told them at the start of the year. Everybody came in to write on it and talk to her. She took the bag off her head and said, "What do you do for the hiccups? I heard. Whoop. Excuse me. You put a bag on your head."

"It's a carbon dioxide signal," he said. "It tells the brain to stop. I forget how it works. Carbon dioxide. I know that part of it."

"So I'm right?"

7

"That's what I heard."

"Okay," she said. She put the bag back over her head and sat up straighter. "Have a seat."

Petey sat down at her desk chair and looked up her skirt. She was sitting on everybody's name. That was exciting too. And the beginnings of her thighs were long. There was something terrific about long muscles like that. Her head was in the brown wrinkled bag but he had to look away anyhow. He said, "How's life?"

"I'm having fun," she said. "How's Petey?"

"Dynamite," he said.

She said, "Bang." She took the bag off her head and shook her hair. It was short and light brown. If you held a jar of honey up to the light in the Great American Market it would be the same color as Miz Bean's hair. She pinched the bag in her fingers and blew into it. When it was full she hiccupped. Then she punched the bag and it exploded. He jumped and got mad. She said, "Dynamite." She smiled. She hiccupped again.

Petey said, "You're supposed to scare yourself, not me."

"Why?"

"Then you get rid of the hiccups."

"Did I scare you?"

"No."

"Oh. Well, how do you suppose somebody could scare himself?"

"Easy," he said.

"How?"

"I don't know. But easy. You know. Tell yourself something bad or something."

"But wouldn't you know it was coming? Wouldn't you know what you were going to do?"

"Sometimes it doesn't matter. You can still surprise yourself."

"How would you do it, Petey?"

"I'll think about it," he told her.

"Okay. I stopped my hiccups."

"How?"

"Talking to you, I guess. Thinking about you. Are you something scary?" She was smiling.

"I'll think about it."

There were three girls to avoid when he went up to industrial arts. He avoided two. He saw the third and blushed. He hid some of the blush with his hand and felt all right. They were soldering. They were unrolling flux and soldering tin cans together that they had cut apart with metal shears the day before. The smell reminded Petey of the taste of the barrel of his father's gun. There was math and science left. Eighth grade wasn't completely like prison because he was allowed to eat dinner at home and when he walked in the halls there were tits to look at. He was ashamed of every street he had walked on in Brooklyn looking tough before his mother canned them and his father retired and went upstate to live in the middle of Christ knows where and herd the cornheads and piggies around the central school. He was ashamed because there had been all those tits and there were all these tits now and he really didn't understand a good deal about them. And there was still math and then something about rivers in science. He wanted the East River under the subway bridge when you went to the city from the Foster Avenue Station in Brooklyn. Then there was study hall and he could do some homework that Miz Carver had given them. Discuss the mechan-

ics of compromise. Surely. You put your cum here and
her mize over there. Your *pro* on the other hand. He
smelled his skin burning and made noises before he
knew he would. They loaded him up with yellow gunk
and a gauze bandage in the nurse's office and then he
went to math. He thought it served him right for talking about cum like he knew something. His hand was
beating. In the car going home he said it was a dumb
accident and nothing much and he was fine. Pop didn't
believe him. When they were back in the house he
unwrapped it and put more ointment on and Petey
was glad he did.

It was hot and there was nobody around. The kids
down the road had farm chores for a while. He probably wouldn't have played with them if they'd come
knocking. The kids up the road prayed and sat in their
blue-white skin at the outside of their trailer. So he
went out past the small barn to their pond to wade
with his sore hand in the air. Pop came too. He looked
tough but he always took care of you. You didn't go
swimming without him there even if you were thirteen and built big like Pop. He sat in an old rocker
with a cane seat that he kept at the side of the pond.
He drank his bourbon and chewed on the ice and
watched. He usually watched you. When he didn't
watch he was listening. He thought about things and
let his belly sag. In school he held it in. That was a
little sad. Petey understood trying to look good,
though. He thought it might help if Pop got his hair
styled.

Pop cooked dinner and Petey washed the dishes.
They both dried them and they talked about the end

of baseball season and the beginning of football season. Petey liked the Yankees and a lot of creeps in school hated them because they were from New York. Pop loved the Mets because Gil Hodges had taken them all the way in the World Series and he had played first base for the Dodgers at Ebbets Field. Pop talked a lot about Ebbets Field and Bedford Avenue. It was almost the end of September. It was still hot but the Mets weren't and the Yanks weren't so it was time to talk about the Buffalo Bills and the Giants and the Jets and big-time football. They split up after dinner. They always did. Petey went up to his room to do his homework. He did it fast and well enough to get by and not amaze anyone with dumbness. He got Bs and Cs. His father told him Cs weren't good enough for college. Petey said he didn't care about college. But he did. He had heard enough from Pop about guys on the force who didn't go to college so they had to get shot because that was the only skill they had. Pop had gone to John Jay at night and during one summer and he had gotten a part of his master's degree at N.Y.U. He always said he'd gotten the worst part of the master's degree. Petey knew he had almost all of it. Pop wanted to be a teacher and he couldn't. That was why he worked in a school and spent time kicking ass on the guys who were mouthing off at teachers. Petey knew that and so did Pop. They talked about each other to each other sometimes when things were good in the house and no one was shouting. They trusted each other sometimes. Petey was upstairs doing his homework. Pop was reading maps again. Petey heard them rustle. Sound carried up through the grids laid into the floor of every room that let the heat rise upstairs in winter from the wood stove in the kitchen and the hot water radiators in the living room.

When he was done, Petey went into the extra bedroom they called their TV room. He turned on the set and waited for Pop to call. Pop called, "You all done with your homework?"

"All done, Pop."

"You did it carefully?"

"Very carefully."

"What'd you have?"

"Math, social slops, English."

"What's social slops?"

"Social *studies*."

"So say it, Petey. God. Social slops. It sounds like some kind of garbage."

"You got it."

"Hey."

"Social studies, Pop."

"What're you watching?"

"What?"

"What're you *watch*ing?"

"'Strike Force.'"

"What's that?"

Petey knew what was coming. "Cops," he said. "Cops, fast cars, girls in tight clothes with big behinds, and everybody carries magnum pistols. I'll change the channel."

"You better change the channel."

"I said I was changing it."

"And the tone of your voice."

"Sorry."

"Okay."

He changed the channel and then Pop's voice came up through the floor and the grate. "Is it good, the cop thing?"

"It's junk," Petey said. "But the girls are dynamite and there's this one detective, he carries a service revolver that must weigh about twenty-six pounds."

"Okay."

"Okay I can watch it?"

"Okay you can watch it. Then you go to bed when it's over."

"Thanks, Pop."

"Thanks for junk. You're welcome for junk."

Petey knew that when Pop told him to go to bed it meant that Pop was falling asleep soon. That meant a night of travel for Pop. He fell asleep early on the sofa. Then he woke up and he made noises like somebody with their head under water. Then he turned the lights out and he went upstairs. Then he woke up in the middle of the night and he went in to read a while on the sofa in the TV room. Then he fell asleep. Sometimes he woke up later and went downstairs and fell asleep on the living room sofa. Once Petey found him asleep in a rocking chair in the kitchen. He never knew where he'd find him in the morning. Sometimes he was afraid he wouldn't find him. Sometimes he was afraid that Pop would be dead when he found him. A tall tough woman dressed up to look like a man went around stabbing people. She was a sexy-looking woman, Petey thought. Her chest was too flat, though. A deodorant commercial came on. Petey sniffed his pits. Heavy stench.

When he turned the TV off he put his pajamas on. He went down past the living room and listened for his father snoring. He heard him. Pop wouldn't wake up for a couple of hours. It was the only time he really went under deep when he slept. So Petey brushed his teeth and went into the pantry for the pot. He squatted and unrolled the gray cloth. It felt heavy every time even though it was small. He always thought that, how heavy it was. It was black and very heavy. There was a lot of stuff concentrated in there. He had the cartridge in his pajama pocket. Pop kept the cartridges upstairs but Petey had sneaked one to keep in his underwear drawer. The gun didn't click out loud like the guns on TV. Everything it did was soft and heavy. He pushed the slide and turned his hand and the drum swung out sideways. It had six black empty holes and they showed up quietly. He dropped the cartridge into one of them and pushed it with his thumb. In his bare feet he went outside. He carried the gun with the chambers still lying sideways to the rest of it. He made sure the safety was on. He went across the road and over the fence and up their hill. They had moved there four months ago and Pop had never climbed the hill he owned. He looked at maps and read books and watched a little TV and fell asleep. Petey wondered if his father ever got laid. He thought of Miz Bean and his father. He was hoping that old guys didn't whack off but he wasn't sure. The grass was cold. The weather was changing. There was fog up on the hill. Or it was a cloud. He couldn't see stars. About two hundred trillion insects kept making the same one noise. It was like standing next to the ocean at Riis Park. The same owl that lived in what was supposed to be a butternut tree made the same noises it made every night. It sounded the same and Petey had the same feeling. It sounded like an old man right next to him who was trying to scare him. It was wet in between his toes now. He had to lean into the hill to keep his balance. After a while he was up. He was breathing hard a little. The knee that knocked him off the track team was sore. He used to hate being on the track team.

He waited around at the top of the hill but he couldn't see anything in the fog and he couldn't think of anything to think about. It was like that every time. He kept waiting for something important. The fog was wet all over his face. Maybe it was a cloud. It touched his cheek like a hand. Bullshit. The only thing that touched your cheek like a hand was a hand. His father used to run the back of his hand along Petey's cheek when he was smaller. He used to do that and look at him. Once in a while he still did it. Petey would stand there and let him. What the hell. And when his mother left she did that. She did it with the ends of her fingers. He remembered that he closed his eyes and when he opened them he saw that her eyes were closed. This time he didn't sit or lie down. He stood on top of their hill. He breathed the fog in. It didn't taste like anything except cold. He closed the gun up. This time it made a low click. He spun the chambers. They didn't spin very far. He did it again and then once more. The cylinder was heavy. The safety was above the trigger guard. He slid it off and put the gun into his mouth and gagged on it. Then he pushed the trigger with his thumb. It didn't feel right with his thumb. He put his index finger into the guard and squeezed off and nothing happened. He hadn't heard the hammer fall. He took the gun out and wiped it on his pajamas. Then he remembered that he might have forgotten to roll the drum when he did it the second time. That cuts your odds down, he thought. Or did it? He was terrible in math. Maybe it helped. "Who gives a shit?" he said out loud. The insects near him cut out for three seconds and then they cut right back in. "Me neither," he said. He put the safety on and went down the hill.

Inside, he heard his father snoring. He wrapped the gun in the cloth and put it back in the pot. He turned the pantry light off and went upstairs. He put the cartridge in his underwear drawer. He got into bed. He got out and went downstairs. He brushed his teeth. Then he went back up. He was reading *Hondo* by Louis L'Amour. It was his favorite book. The tough man sleeping outside with his dog named Dog to protect the kid and his mother. The mother was beautiful. They slept together and they did it. His father would have said "Made love," and then gone red. He put his hands on his balls but it didn't feel right about the Louis L'Amour woman. She was a mother. He thought about Miz Bean but that didn't feel right either. He thought about Miz Carver in History and that was all right. She had terrific tits and she knew kids looked at them. Pop said she was smart. But she had those terrific tits. Later on he heard Pop come up out of sleep. He made noises and then he just groaned. He came upstairs. He walked on the steps like a crippled old man. Petey liked it more when Pop was sleeping upstairs. He heard Pop's bed at the other end of the hall. He heard the bed and then Pop made a noise like something hurt him. Then the house was quiet and Petey could feel himself letting go of everything. It was like dropping off the board at the YMCA swimming pool except that it's dark. You never reach the water. You keep on falling. You know you won't get hurt.

The hot weather stopped and so did the swimming. After school on Friday he stayed outside and kicked the football from the road to the hedgerow at the end of the side yard. Then he kicked it back at the road. When it bounced he ran at it and jumped on top of it and held on against tacklers. He landed slam on top of the ball with his stomach. He was trying to breathe. He couldn't. He could feel the sweat on his face. Pop called to him, "Lie back. Lie back and wait. You can breathe."

He put his knees up and let his head go back. The sky looked like wood smoke. The light behind it was yellow and flickery. But it was mostly smoky air and then Pop's big face came like a balloon. It drifted in there and the eyes looked down. Then it drifted away. He got up and breathed. He took his shoe and sock off and looked for Pop. He was sitting on the side in his lawn chair. He had a bowl for ice and a squat glass and a bottle. His legs looked skinny. They were crossed. He was slumped in the chair. He was watching. So Petey rolled his pants leg up twice and started kicking from the roadside back to the hedgerow. The ball didn't go that far but it got high sometimes and it sometimes rolled a good distance. He kept on running and jumping for it after he kicked. His foot stung but it didn't hurt when he kicked. After the kick it would sting but he ran and jumped and kicked anyway.

He heard ice and bourbon and his father's voice. His father was sitting in the lawn chair at the side of the field like an audience. His father kept on talking. After a while Petey tuned in.

"Relationship," Pop said.

"Excuse me?"

"No, you keep kicking it. I can talk over the sound of your hooves. Do you have a reason for doing it with your shoe off?"

"Barefoot kickers kick it better. They get paid more."

"You intend to be a professional barefoot football kicker?"

"I thought maybe I could get a college scholarship."

"Wouldn't you have to go out for the high-school football team first?"

"I'm not ready this year."

"You need practice?"

"Yeah."

"You could practice with the team."

"I'm not ready yet."

"Yes. That's what Lizzie says about me and her also."

"The barefoot part?"

Pop rattled his ice around. "The ready part."

"Oh."

"No, she means she thinks I need some time alone. And with you. But not married or anything. You know."

Petey tore off to the hedgerow and recovered an on-sides kick. He tore-ass back and barely got the nose across the goal line before the defenders caught him from behind and caved him in. But he scored. He carried the ball loose and trotted back to the bench. Pop was saying, "Several times. And I guess you *would* say that about her. *I'll* say it about her and welcome to it. How do you do." Pop lifted the glass and drank and grinned. Pop was getting plowed. Petey was glad. He was funny when he was drunk. He smiled and he never shouted. Later on he apologized a lot and felt terrible. Guilty, Petey always said to him after he had gotten drunk. Guilty as charged.

Pop said, "Well, of course I told her that open and honest and well-modulated relationships are fine. I like to modulate them about once a week, except during the snow season of course, when you want to watch out for creosote and other kinds of buildup. I told her how we could skip a weekend from time to time because dating is largely overrated for a man of my increasing age and decreasing stamina. I didn't sound at all funny that time either. Did you really ask me about this?"

Petey said, "Sure."

"I thought you did. Did I tell you to?"

"Didn't have to. And I didn't have to ask. You just started in telling."

"That's me. A sergeant of detectives and almost a lieutenant and a complete gentleman. And something of a patsy, don't you think."

"I didn't know you were *dating* Miz Bean. You know. Going together."

Pop nodded and rattled the ice. "Lizzie Bean and I have been something of an item in the nonsmoking section of the teachers' room. The nonsmokers have had to speculate. The smokers hit the bars for a beer now and again, so they see us there."

"I didn't know you were *going* with her."

"I should have told you."

"You should have, Pop."

"Thank you. When it got serious, I would have told you."

"When?"

"Now. It just got serious. Now. Except you can't nag me for not telling. *You* don't tell *me* a lot. You don't always pay attention to a lot that isn't about you."

"That's how teenagers are supposed to be."

"I know. That's why I didn't tell you."

"Do you love her?"

His father looked at him very long. Petey was getting ready to go back and kick the ball. "I love you. You and I live together. Mom loves you too."

"She lives someplace else."

"She has to. She's pretty sure she loves another man."

"If she loves another man, she can love another kid. If she doesn't love you anymore, she can also not love me anymore. Don't you read the scuzzy books they leave all over the media center and the guidance office? Miz Bean gives them out to everybody. That's the major fear for adolescents and younger children during a divorce."

"Listen," Pop said, bending down over his gut to pour more bourbon. "Listen, are we talking about me and my love life or you and your teenage torments?"

"Just talk about Miz Bean."

"You watch your mouth. I hear lust in your voice."

"It's a preparation for adult life, Pop."

"I hate that word, *adult*. She uses it a lot. A mature, adult relationship. What it means—it means this guy from Long Island used to date her, he's driving up for a weekend of rural jollies. Mulvaney's his name. They're gonna sit around and analyze each other. She studied with him. He's an old guy. But not old enough. And he's very literate. She told me that. You like it? Literate. Guess what that makes me."

"You got your master's degree, Pop."

"Just the hind legs of it, kid. Come on."

"I'll make dinner," Petey said.

Pop smiled. "What do you plan on cooking?"

"Bacon and eggs?"

"No bacon."

"Eggs?"

"Fried. Over. Cooked hard."

"I was thinking scrambled, with milk mixed in, cooked soft."

"You were thinking how you could force me to come down off the booze and make you something good."

"We could have a Jack Daniels omelet," Petey said.

"I'm thinking Italian sweet sausage with peppers and onions fried in, poured hot over big spiral noodles so the olive oil smokes your mouth."

"No garlic," Petey said.

"One clove."

"Deal."

Petey stuck his hand out. Pop grabbed hold. They pretended that Petey could pull him up and out of his chair. They left the ice and the football and a sock and a shoe on the grass. Petey came back for them. He knew he wouldn't be going out that night. When he came back in, Pop was mincing garlic and slicing onions. He had the telephone tucked under his chin while he worked. He was talking to Miz Carver about history. "I'm still a kind of detective," he said. His voice was low and fake. "I still like to look for things."

So she was there with them on Saturday. Petey was

outside and they were inside drinking coffee and looking at maps. Petey was rolling loads of firewood in a
wheelbarrow from the pile outside of the barn to the
inside, where he stacked it. The wood had been deliv-
ered in a dump truck. It smelled good and it looked
orange and white like soft stuff. It was very hard and
very heavy. Petey like making it into stacks that didn't
fall. Miz Carver was inside with her famous chest. He
loaded the wheelbarrow and then unloaded it and he
kept the stacks even and straight.

He didn't need to hear them. Pop talked about maps
because he needed something to worry about, Petey
figured. He needed a job that nobody would do. On
the maps there was a little cluster of dots off the high-
way and up in the hills. It was called Sweet River these
days. On the old map that Pop had bought in a garage
sale the same place was called Negro Hollow. The map
was dated 1943. Pop asked people on their road and
they called it Nigger Holler.

One of them had been driving a dark brown pickup.
He had leaned out to look at Pop. The man's face had
been dirty, the way a kid's face gets dirty and stays that
way all day. His teeth had been brown. He'd said,
"Nigger Holler?"

Pop had said, "You've got blacks around here?"

"*I* ain't got one," the man in the truck had said. "I
heard about some. I doubt they'd stay here."

"Where would they live?"

"You looking for some?"

"I'm just asking you something." Petey had known
Pop would just as soon open the door and pull the man
out and step on his face. He had known that in two
more questions Pop would tear the door off first and

then step on him. But Pop had smiled. His face had gone red. His big ears had gotten darker. Petey hated that smile. It meant you got embarrassed in a shopping mall or a movie house because Pop was losing his temper. It meant Pop might stick his face into Petey's or someone else's and his breath would hiss when he said whatever was choking him. It would be like putting your face over a kettle when the steam came out.

"Okay must of ran them off twenty years ago if they stayed that long," the man had said. He'd put the truck in gear. Pop's face was wrinkled. He was trying to figure out what the man meant. "You be needing to look someplace else, then," the man had said. He had driven away.

Pop read the maps. He took books out of the high-school library and the town library. He asked old people questions. He looked for clues off and on. But this Saturday he was really being a detective. Petey thought Pop was probably feeling up Miz Carver while Petey stacked their winter's wood. He wondered if Pop would start in wearing his gun again since he had started playing detective with Miz Carver. He wheeled about a dozen big chunks in and dumped them on the barn's cement floor. He set each chunk of log on the stack. He rocked every log once it was on the woodpile so he knew it wouldn't fall. The logs smelled like the ground under rocks. They smelled cold. They smelled old. He wondered where Pop would put the gun when he took it off at night.

❧   ❧   ❧

Back in Brooklyn there were streets with easy names. He didn't know what they were named after. But they were easy to remember. Nostrand Avenue. Newkirk Avenue. Cortelyou Road. Dorchester Road. Up here when they rode in the car they came to places that mostly didn't have signs on the road. The roads were mostly dirt or blacktop with potholes. Sometimes they did have signs but you could never remember them. It was like meeting new people. You forgot their names right away. Grant Follet Road. White Store Bridge Road. Bowers Almstead Road. Pop was getting to know them, though. He was really interested. He never got lost. Petey never knew where they were going. Pop could always get them back home. With Miz Carver in the front seat and Petey in the back Pop was going to Sweet River. He called it Nigger Holler. Miz Carver said Negro Hollow. They were going to try to find the Nigger Holler Church. It was on the old map but it wasn't on the new one. Petey was thinking about a movie called *The Land That Time Forgot*. Only half the expedition got out of this valley that was about a half a million years younger than everyplace else. Most of the expedition got eaten by a wild Tyrannosaurus rex and these cave people who sucked the marrow out of modern people's bones. *Stay on the map*, he thought.

The road was bumpy as hell. They went past the usual shitboxes and places that never got painted. There were trailers all over the place. Some of the farms were big and there was green and yellow John Deere equipment in some fields. But most of them were terrible little shacks with paper and tires and pieces of car all over the lawns. It wasn't that cold but smoke came out of a lot of the chimneys. When they went past he smelled the smoke. It was like a taste of something good. The road dipped and then came up. Pasture land was all grown over with bushes off to their right. There was a dirt road that went into the hills behind the pastures. On their left was a tiny red house all boarded up. "That should be School Number Eleven," Pop said.

"How'd you like to teach in *that?*" Miz Carver said. Petey imagined her breasts squeezed against the chalkboard. She was looking at one of Pop's old maps. She was calling out the names of the dirt roads and some of the buildings.

They climbed away from the shitboxes and trailers and dirt roads. For a little while they were on blacktop and then it was rocks and dirt. The road got wider. There was a stream below the roadbed to the right. It had mostly dried up. The forest was back from the road. There was a horrible house made of thin boards nailed in every direction. It was green-brown and it looked like the air blew through it. A school bus painted blue was in the side yard. Dogs ran next to the car and barked. A little baby in a shirt and no pants stood on the lawn and watched. The place looked like everyone else who used to live there was dead.

The road got wider. There weren't any houses. The forest was farther back from the road. Petey thought they were in a new country. Then there was a very small house on the left. It was painted shiny brown. It wasn't too much bigger than a big truck. It had small windows that were square at the bottom and pointed at the top. One of the windows had colored glass. There wasn't any steeple but Petey knew it was the church. So did Pop. He stopped a ways down from it and they looked. Miz Carver said to him, "Why do you want to do this so much?"

Pop said, "It's good to be looking for something. It's what a lot of my job used to be."

"But *what?*" Miz Carver said.

"Doesn't matter all that much," Pop said.

Petey said *Bullshit,* but just to himself.

Pop turned the motor off but the dogs had heard it. All three of them were down there at the car. They looked like they never ate. They were howling and showing their teeth and looking hungry. Miz Carver pushed the doorlock button with her elbow. A scrawny woman came out of the church. She looked like she didn't eat either. Pop opened the door. One of the dogs came up. Petey thought Pop was going to kick it for a field goal. He bent over a little and said, "Hello." The dog barked once more and then backed up and got quiet. All of a sudden Petey wanted them to get a dog.

Pop went to the woman like a cop. Petey thought he was going to take out his notebook and write things down or show her his shield. But all he did was smile and bend over to her a little. He pointed at the house and then the car. When she looked over Petey waved. She didn't wave back. She looked at Pop and then she nodded and then she shook her head. Pop shrugged. The woman shrugged. Pop came back to the car and waved to the woman. A little girl in a long silvery nightgown came to the door of the church. The woman shouted at her. The girl ran inside. They drove away going uphill. Pop said, "Nothing."

Miz Carver said, "She hasn't found any documents?"

Pop said, "She knew it was the church and she even went to the library, she said, and looked up about it."

"Looked up about it," Miz Carver said. "It's like another country up here."

"Yeah," Pop said. "Except it isn't. It's the same one. That's the exciting part."

"And she didn't find anything?" Miz Carver said.

"We didn't either," Pop said.

Miz Carver said, "Looked up about it."

"There's an altar platform inside," Pop said. "She said there was a little railing and room for about ten or fifteen people."

"And that was where the Negroes came to pray," Miz Carver said.

"Yeah. But why were they here? I mean *here?* This isn't hospitable territory."

She said, "Once it wasn't that bad. The Underground Railroad stopped here. It wasn't all that bad."

Petey thought of a train on dark tracks going into a tunnel and coming out in The Land That Time Forgot.

"Couldn't be all that good," Pop said.

"Look," Miz Carver said. "You're an Irish cop. You used to be. In the city. Everybody knows about Irish cops. They're bigots. They hate everybody. Negroes, Jews, Protestants. Everyone. So how come you're on the trail of these black people who probably don't exist?"

Pop was laughing. When he stopped he said, "Some of my best friends were bigots. But my mother was also a Jew."

"That makes you *Jew*ish," Miz Carver said. She was excited. "In Israel, anyhow. You'd be a Jew."

"In Auschwitz too," Pop said. "Same deal. But I'm

an Irish cop. I was raised Irish Catholic. I even look like one."

Petey said *I'm not a Jew,* but not out loud.

Pop sounded like he'd heard him anyway. "It probably wouldn't be that easy up here, being Jewish."

"That wouldn't stop *you,*" Miz Carver said. Petey thought about throwing up.

"No. I'm an Irish cop," Pop said. "I used to be. I just like looking for things. I like the rules of it and I like to look. You're the history expert. So help me look, will you?"

If he wasn't there they'd be doing it, Petey thought. Then he figured they might be working on it anyway. They drove to Burger King and then they went back home. They dropped him off. They were going to the county office building to check on land records. They were investigating the church. They left. Petey knew they were going back to Miz Carver's apartment in town. The county offices were closed on Saturday and everybody knew it. "I'm a cop's *kid,* for Chrissakes," Petey said to the outside of his house.

He didn't go in. He went to the barn and worked on stacking more wood. He knew he'd be thinking about his mother soon. He didn't want to. But he would. He would settle for being miserable if she told him it wasn't easy letting him go away with Pop. Some of his friends were in divorces. The parents always fought about who got the kids. The mothers always won. Once a father had won. Burris's father won. But Burris's mother was crazy. She washed her hands so much they had to pack them in ointment and put rubber gloves on her. Otherwise fathers didn't get to keep their kids in a divorce. So his mother gave him away. He couldn't figure out how she could do that. He knew he wasn't wonderful. He was an asshole sometimes. He was selfish. He had a lousy temper with her that he used to lose sometimes. It would blow up on him. It reminded him of Pop. It felt good and it scared him. He didn't have it with Pop. Probably Pop was too tough for him. But he used to be lousy with his mother sometimes. But he couldn't believe how she was able to let him go. He was an okay kid otherwise, he figured. Besides. She used to hug him a lot. She kissed him goodnight and she kissed him goodbye and sometimes she kissed him hello. So it was pretty much of a surprise that she wouldn't put up a fight about keeping him in the house with her wherever she'd moved to. He wondered what kind of street she lived on. He was crying. He was totally pissed off that he was crying. It was humiliating to be his age and cry. He stopped. He could do that. He stopped. He blew his nose with just his fingers the way the cornheads did it outside school. He built up the rows of wood. He made them perfect. Miz Bean had said to him one time, "When you feel that bad, it's a kind of energy. Push something with it." He didn't know what she thought he was feeling bad about or how she'd known. But he remembered. He stacked the wood. He didn't think it was going to help that much.

Late that afternoon Pop came home without Miz Carver. Petey was surprised. His father was lonely and he always did something about everything. When he felt something he acted back at the feeling. But Pop came home to be lonely alone. Petey was outside the barn. He wasn't stacking. He was looking at the stones. He was building a wall with them. It was the kind of wall he saw in pastures near old houses. He laid the stones on top of each other and put small round ones into the spaces where the flat ones left room. He knew that was called chinking. Pop came out of the house with a sweater over his shoulders and a sweatshirt for Petey and some drinks. He put the sweater on and then he stood behind Petey and tied the sleeves of the sweatshirt around Petey's waist. He got a folding chair from inside the barn and carried it back far enough so he could sit and drink and watch Petey work.

Pop sat a while and sipped. Then he said, "Why'd you leave those two big flat ones out?"

Petey said, "I'm saving them for corners at the end."

"Is that what they mean by cornerstone?"

"I don't know. I guess maybe. I don't know."

"That must be what cornerstone means. Well, I'll be damned. Listen. This wall you built—are you intending to fence the barn in with it?"

Petey was lifting rocks. "No."

"Or out?"

"I guess not," Petey said.

"You're just building up a wall, are you?"

Petey set the stone down and said, "I guess I quit for a while."

Pop gave him the can of Coke he'd carried out and he pointed to the sweatshirt. Petey untied it and put it on. He drank the Coke while they looked at the wall.

"It's beautiful," Pop said. "It's a beautiful damned wall. I wish I could build something that safe."

Petey looked up. He smiled for the word *safe*.

"It's beautiful," Pop said.

Petey sat down on the ground next to his chair. Pop crossed his legs. He sighed back into the wind. It was coming over the pond. Petey smelled the weeds from the far end of the pond. He couldn't remember what his mother did this time of the afternoon on Saturday. He wondered who his mother loved now. He looked at Pop. Pop was looking through Petey's eyes and into his brain. He sometimes did that and that was when he looked the most like a cop. That was when Petey wanted to say: *Pig!* He looked away. He couldn't remember anything. Pop's arm came out around his waist. He pulled Petey into his side. The metal arm of the chair bit him but he stayed there.

"Beautiful," Pop said.

Then they cleaned up and went in. Pop made another drink and they chopped onions and cheese and mixed them into hamburger meat and broiled the burgers up. They made a bag of frozen french fries and then they went to the movies. Petey saw girls he knew who were dating with older kids. He was ashamed about something all through the movie. He didn't know what it was. It had to do with the girls. He didn't want to leave until after they did. Pop knew that. Before the lights went on he put his hand around Petey's arm and they took off. They got malted milks at the Burger King drive-in window and escaped home. They came up Mason's Road. It went down a little driveway at Mason's smallest barn that was just off the two-lane. The driveway curled around the barn and went over a stone bridge through Mason's lower meadow and up. They drove on dirt and rocks until they hit the crest. You could see everything from there. The sky was black. The farms and shitboxes were dark. You couldn't see stars or cars or airplanes. For a couple of seconds it felt like they were the only people in the world. Then the road started looking at them. Green eyes came up from the road and floated around looking at them. Pop hit the brights. They saw four kittens. Then they saw six altogether. They were jumping. They were soft in the air when they moved. The road was only a road again. There was just dirt and puddles of manure off a spreader and big rocks and brush off to the side. The houses were just places with the lights off. But he knew they were there and people were in them. He leaned against the door. He wondered if Pop was thinking about Miz Bean.

Pop asked, "Do you think the priest did it?"

"What?"

"In the movie. The cop's brother was the priest."

"Yeah, I remember."

"You think the priest was the killer?"

"No. The *cop* thought the priest was the killer. The moviemaker was the killer."

"I thought—"

Petey said, "You really thought the cop was the killer, didn't you?"

"I did?"

"I bet you did."

"Why?"

"Because when you were a cop you kept on talking about this one was taking, that one was taking. Remember? Mom and me used to think every cop we saw in the street was a crook."

"You used to think that way?"

Petey nodded in the darkness. The cats were all around the car. He didn't know why they were parked here at the top of a hill in the middle of some field with a dirt road going over it.

"Shame on you," Pop said. "The cop in the movie was a hero."

"I was talking about the guys in the city."

"Some of them were okay too. *I* was a hero."

"I know."

Pop said, "Nah. Come on, I was joking."

"No," Petey said, "you were."

"I really was, one time," Pop said. "I got a medal."

"I remember when you came home from that with Mom. She was dressed up. I stayed with that girl. The babysitter."

"Linda?"

"That's the one. And you came home and Linda left and Mom started crying. She started hitting you. She said you didn't care if you died. She said anyone who didn't care if they died didn't love the people they were leaving behind. She said you weren't worthy—"

"Come on, that's a lot of crap."

"It is?"

"Don't you think I loved you guys?"

"You didn't love Mom."

"Not that simple."

"You did love her?"

"Not *that* simple."

"And me?"

"Simple."

"So people who don't care if they die do love some of the people they leave behind them?"

33

"Geez, Petey, *I* don't know. Why are—look: if they love them, they love them. The dying doesn't mean that much, I guess."

"It doesn't?"

"I don't think that's true. Dying means a lot." Pop laughed. "I'm not much of a philosopher."

"Which does it?" Petey asked. "Does it mean a lot or not?"

He heard Pop's leather jacket move. "I don't know," Pop said. He sounded sad.

Petey said, "I—to tell you the truth, I don't know either."

Pop moved again in the dark. Petey felt him. He watched the kittens in the road. Pop put the car in gear and the kittens stared. Then they floated off to the side and they were just eyes.

Once they had to stay late after school. Pop had a long meeting with the guidance department. That meant they would sit around and eat doughnuts and talk about the cornheads who smoked dope in the rest rooms. They would discuss the girls who messed around with guys in the printing shop. They would say awful words, Pop had told him. "Puberty." "Socialization." Pop hated the meetings. A lot of the people at them treated him like a janitor, Pop had said. Miz Bean never did. Even when she was going around with other guys.

Petey played basketball in the gym with some of the cornheads while Pop was at the meeting. Mr. Monday the gym teacher was there smoking cigarettes with a real janitor and watching the halfcourt game. Petey was assing the cornheads out so they couldn't position for rebounds. He barely needed to jump. One time he did jump because he felt like laying into someone. He went up off the shot. The rebound came to him like a pass. But he went up anyway. He came down with his legs out and his elbows flying. He tore the ball away and swung around him. A cornhead went down moaning. He got up. He looked at Petey in a funny way. Petey said, "You okay?"

The cornhead said, "That was a foul."

Petey said, "It's only a foul if you can't stop the bleeding or you need to set the bone. That's the only kind of a foul."

The kid looked at him. Petey moved one step closer in case the guy really wanted to dance. But he moved back and told them he was quitting the game. Another cornhead came in. Petey took the ball out, got it back, dribbled to the top of the key and dropped in the high-arc jump shot. When they came out after him the time after that he drove to the hoop. He was bare to the waist. He was running with sweat. He was wishing he had a little hair on his chest for the sweat to slide through. He took one step to the left and took it back. He pivoted. He drove. He stopped. He jumped off the drive and banked it in off the board. His knee was sore but he didn't care. One of the cornheads on his team said, "Any time you need somebody on the same side as you, just give a call, huh?"

Mr. Monday came over when Petey threw the basketball at the cornhead. Petey said to him, "It was a pass."

Monday took Petey into the locker room. He lit another cigarette. It smelled like Miz Bean's. Then the rest of the smell came through and it was like hundred-year-old socks and jocks. Monday said, "How come, you play basketball in gym class, you never hit the boards, you don't box out, you don't drop the long jumpers in like that? You just run around and pass the ball off and sleep standing up? Then, you come in here with some big mean motherfuckers—two of them play varsity for me, you know. And you play the way I just seen you play? How come?"

"Now I know why we don't win any games," Petey said. He was panting from the way he'd just played. He didn't need to, though. He was embarrassed. Breathing hard was something to do.

Monday said, "So how come?"

"I felt like it," Petey said. "Sometimes it's fun."

"To give a little lesson like that?"

"That's playgrounds."

"New York City schoolyard ball," Monday said. He acted like he had heard it too much. He acted bored.

"Brooklyn playgrounds," Petey said. "Wingate Field. Caton Avenue. The big yard across the street from Midwood on Bedford Avenue?"

"*I* don't know," Monday said. "I don't care where you played ball before you came here. What I care is, you played ball with niggers. Didn't you?"

Petey nodded.

"I wish I had a couple of colored boys," Monday said. "You'd be the next best thing. You'll be a freshman next year. You're big. You're mean. You come out, you could start for the varsity. Shoot, you could finish. You could maybe get yourself a decent scholarship. Listen—Syracuse? Great program. Utica? Costello's at Utica, you know. Listen—I know Lou Carne*seca*. You hear me? I *know* him. I'm trying to tell you—St. John's Redmen, national TV. I'm trying to tell you,

you're *good*. You could help me out a lot, you come out."

Petey nodded his head. He smiled. He liked the idea of being the slick black power forward on a team of cornheads. He shook his head.

Monday said, "What? Why *not?*"

Petey said, "I don't like basketball."

He didn't tell Pop when they drove home. It was just about dark. They'd gone to the Italian restaurant in town for dinner. Pop had drunk a little wine. Petey could smell it in the car. He could hear Pop being careful about how he said his words. They went the long way home. That meant Pop wanted to talk. But he didn't. Petey thought maybe Pop was waiting for him to talk. He didn't want to. He wanted to look at the rocks and the grass. Every piece of rock and every blade of grass had its own shadow, that time of day. Petey was looking out the window when Pop stopped the car at the middle of Mason's Road. There was a gully under that part of the road. If you looked just before you turned onto it, you could see how the space under the road where water ran through was built from old tractor tires. There was dirt and rock around them but the tires held the road up.

Pop kept the car running. Then he shut it off and Petey looked up. They were sitting next to the herd of cows that always grazed there. Petey looked at the big plastic tags in their ears. Pop said, "How'd it go today?"

Petey said, "Good." That was what he had said when Pop asked the same question in the restaurant.

"Good," Pop said.

Petey was thinking about the kittens in the road.

37

This was where they had seen them. They had talked about things. He figured Pop was trying to get them talking again. *Puberty,* Petey thought. *Socialization.* He looked at Pop. He didn't look happy. Maybe *Pop* needed to talk, Petey thought. He cocked his head.

Pop said, "What?"

At the fence to their left four deer jumped together. They went across the road about thirty feet in front of the car. They jumped the other fence to get into the meadow on the right. All the cows pivoted around at the same time. They had their heads back and their chests up. Their dugs were flapping. When they wheeled to look the deer stopped and looked back. Nothing moved. Then one of the deer moved. The lead cow moved. The deer jumped and took off. The cattle moved off with them. The deer ran and the cows rocked. They ran parallel to the deer like giant black and white rocking horses. When the deer were out of sight the cows were still rocking along.

Pop roared. He pointed at the cows who were still running for absolutely no reason in the world. Petey started in laughing too. When Pop stopped and wiped his eyes and started the car he reached out and slapped Petey on the leg. He nodded to Pop and Pop nodded back. He was still laughing a little. Petey tried all the way home to think of something to say about the deer and the cows.

A lot of what Pop did just didn't make sense. He dated Miz Carver. She always talked like a voice coming over on the radio. Miz Bean just talked to you. But Pop hung around with Miz Carver or whatever he did with Miz Carver and Miz Bean stayed away. He couldn't figure out why Pop didn't go over to Miz

Bean's house and kick. Pop never took that kind of shit from anyone else. But Miz Bean made him miserable and he let her. He stayed away from her in the halls too. Petey watched for them. They just walked past each other saying "Hi," the way you do when you want to be someplace else with somebody different.

It also didn't make any sense that Pop kept fooling around with Nigger Holler or Negro Hollow or Sweet River. It didn't make sense that he did it to be a detective because they had come up here so Pop could *stop* being a detective. He had said so. But Pop kept looking at old maps. He went to the county offices and looked at deeds of property. He tried to figure out who the guy was who had run the church. Somebody at the Agway finally told him after school one afternoon. He looked like the guy with brown teeth who drove the brown pickup. It turned out to be his brother. He towed a stump grinder behind his truck. His teeth looked better than his brother's. They were in the Agway buying a rake. Then they'd have two rakes and they could get the leaves off the lawn together. The guy with only yellow teeth was in there in his gray overalls and black rubber boots. He had a cigarette in his mouth. Sometimes he took it out so he could talk. Sometimes he let it waggle. The ash dropped off. Petey thought if he smoked cigarettes he would keep them on his lip like that.

"Yupper. Old Tom told me you were inquiring. Sure as shit. We lived next door to Nigger Holler. Lived on the Penbroke Road, down to the Penbroke sisters' farm, nearly. I never did see but one colored there, I don't think. There was this Injun girl never wore shoes to school until after the snow flew. You might count

39

Injuns as coloreds, I don't know." He took the little bit of the cigarette out and squeezed it between two fingers. He watched to see if Petey was watching him do that. Petey looked away. "But there sure as shit was a church there. Still *is* there. Real nice gal lives there all alone. No, I'm lying to you. Lives with a baby or two, as I recall it. Well. It was a church back then. White folks went there, of course, not colored, on account of there wasn't but one colored in the district by then. You remember me telling you that? But older folks knew from back when there was. Said there always was a white preacher, I believe. Free Methodist, seems to me. He was a good American. He sent his only daughter over to England and she cured England of the whooping cough. Apparently that was a terrible affliction in that part of the world. Wasn't ever much of a treat over *here*, now that I mention it."

Petey had tried staying home from school with the whooping cough when his folks were having some bad fights. He came downstairs grabbing at his throat and stomach. He coughed so hard he made himself dizzy. His mom knew what he was doing. She held onto him with her cold hands. She kissed him. She cried. She made him walk to school, though. He was still dizzy. He told the nurse he had the whooping cough. He whooped for her and he fainted. They sent for his mom. She came over in her raincoat and loafers and an old hat that was too big. It was Pop's. Her face looked white. She said, "Didn't you do a great job of it, Petey. You *deserve* to stay home for that." In the car she said, "Don't tell." She drove them to Wilner's. They were the only two people in there on all that marble floor. They sat at the soda fountain and she ordered two giant root beers. They slurped through their straws. She looked at him. She was crying those huge slow tears while she slurped. It gave her the hiccups. Now he was wishing that he'd known about the paper bag so he could have helped her stop. But she had kept on doing it.

There was whispering in school by dopers and the carheads who had grease cemented in under their fingernails. Somebody had trashed some teacher's desk. Pop was walking around with his cop look on Monday afternoon. He was on the balls of his feet with his back rounded and his belly out a little. It was the cop look that said: I'm just walking around and don't pay any attention to *me*. It was different when he stood on his toes and stuck his chest out and lifted up his chin and turned red. That was before he took somebody down and hurt them. This was the one where he looked like he didn't matter. He never didn't matter. He was walking around like that. His two cop looks got confused when Miz Bean went past because Pop turned red and forgot to look innocent. But he also forgot to look dangerous. He looked like Petey, Petey thought.

Tuesday morning they got in late. That was because at the guidance department meeting on Monday Pop was bossed by Miz Bean. Petey knew he wasn't going to be fun afterwards. He wasn't. They had come home late on Monday afternoon and Pop had had his drink while they cooked. It had been cold and they had stayed inside and everything had folded up on everything else like an accordion. Nobody had told jokes before they'd gone to bed. Petey had stayed in his room. He'd been tired from playing basketball. He'd been tired from hanging around school alone while he waited for Pop. In the late afternoon in November the school was dark green because of the floors and the funny light. He'd been alone in the school, it felt like. He'd been underwater, it felt like. He'd spent his time and then everything had folded up after a while at home.

He went right to his locker on Tuesday morning when they got to school late. There was a funny noise coming from up the hall. It was like somebody pushing on the top of your head or on your shoulders. It wasn't heavy and it didn't hurt but it was there and different from the air. It was people talking a certain way. When he got there just when the homeroom bell was ringing he knew he didn't have to go to homeroom right away because of the way people talked. Mr. Zacharias the principal was standing with his hands in the pockets of his weird gray suit with the red stripes running all directions on it. He looked like he was crying. He looked ready to cry, anyway. Petey saw that Miz Demeter the librarian was crying for real. There was a sheriff's deputy with his hand on his gun. He was wearing a wide-brimmed hat. There was a trooper from the State Police. He wasn't wearing any hat. He had blond hair in curls that looked like it was wet. He had white teeth. He was smiling at Miz Demeter and Miz Bean and Pop and the president of the Student Council who was crying too. Mr. Ferguson from wood shop was pushing people back and forth. But they stayed pretty much inside the library or right outside the doors. Mr. Monday, who coached everything except volleyball, was pushing people one way but they kept bumping into the people Mr. Ferguson was pushing the other way. Miz Demeter kept starting to cry again. Miz Bean was shoving her feet into the file cards on the floor. Pop looked around and picked up some cards. He put them down again.

So somebody had trashed the library. Somebody had torn it up. Some of the dumb posters about how great you feel when you read were hanging off the corkboards by one thumbtack. Miz Demeter's famous sign about needing passes to stay there was in four parts. The wires were unplugged from the computers. The TV monitor was on its screen. It looked like a fat man on his belly. Most of the books were on the shelves but a lot weren't. All the drawers of the catalogues were pulled out and they looked like somebody slid them all over the floor. Two of the drawers were just emptied out near the cabinet. Lots of the cards were sprayed all the hell over the place. A lot of drawers were empty. Pop was walking around on his toes with his shoulders down. He was looking at everything. Petey was going to back up and go to class. But he kept watching Pop. He smiled. There went Pop.

All day everybody kept passing the library even when they didn't need to. Miz Bean was talking to Miz Demeter one time. One time Miz Bean clapped her hands and said, "God damn it, but let's go on and—" One time Pop was in there on his hands and knees like a detective in a movie. One time DiStefano was there with a bunch of his cornhead friends. He was saying, "It's better when they piss on the books and burn some of them. There was this school outside Syracuse, they threw these dead chickens all over the place and took turns barfing on them. Really." One time Miz Bean was talking to Pop and he was looking down at her and listening and then talking back. She

43

was shaking her head and watching him. Then she smiled.

After lunch everybody was talking about the roller skating party to raise money for the Student Council. Lugene Winton walked like she was on roller skates all the time. She came up to Petey and stood in front of him and all he could do was blush. She told him he should have a date for the party if he dared to show his face on Saturday night. He didn't know why she was getting tough with him. She was as tall as he was. She was taller than he was. She leaned over around the books she held on her chest. She was making herself look smaller. So he finally understood. He said, "How could I get a date, Lugene?" He even made his face smile, he figured.

She looked right along his nose and up and into his eyes. She kept waiting.

He said, "The bell just rang."

Lugene closed her eyes. She had freckles she said she hated. He looked at them. She opened her eyes. His cheeks hurt and under his ears it felt the way it does when you eat something sour. She said, "I can't believe how immature you are, Peter. How juvenile can you *get?*"

DiStefano said from behind him, "*I* don't know. *How* juvenile can he get?"

Mr. Staschauer the English teacher took them into his father's office for fighting. DiStefano was holding onto his left wrist and was limping. Pop looked at them and said, "Get out. You're both on warning of in-school suspension. One false move and you're dead. Go to class. Go to *school*, for Chrissakes. I got a wrecked library and you zoo brains are picking fights." His voice was thick and low. Petey was in trouble at home, he knew. He told DiStefano. He also told him he would probably have to be killed later on if Petey had time.

DiStefano asked him to make an appointment. Petey kicked him in the ankle that was hurt. DiStefano screamed his name out and Petey took off because they were too close to Pop's office. "No balls at *all*," DiStefano shouted. Petey figured he was right.

They got home later on Tuesday afternoon than on Monday. Pop was so mad he made a drink while he was still in his school clothes. He sat down in the kitchen and crossed his legs and drank. He went for another one. He carried it upstairs while he changed his clothes. "Hot dogs," Pop said. "I can't think what to cook. Hot dogs. You cook 'em, Petey. You know all about hot dogs, don't you? Fighting in the halls like trash. *You* cook." Pop added a little bit more bourbon and tucked the flannel shirt around his belly and went into the living room and sat. Petey made hot dogs and sauerkraut and baked beans with floppy bacon on top and mustard mixed in. He poured out milk for himself and a beer for Pop and called him and they ate in the kitchen without talking.

Pop kept looking at him. Petey looked at his beans. It was the world's longest dinner with two people at the table in the State of New York. Petey went upstairs to look for the address of the judges of the *Guinness Book of World Records* and to work on his assignments. Pop talked on the telephone to Miz Carver. Petey could hear from what Pop said that Miz Carver wanted to come over to do more research. Petey put his hand on his lap. Research. Miz Carver was telling Pop something and Pop said it back to her: "Dark Valley. That's a hell of a thing, isn't it? Dark Valley. I like knowing that. Thank you. Thank you for that. Dark Valley. Little place with a lot of names and no black folks, huh? Dark Valley. Uh-huh." They talked a while. Pop used his phony voice pretty soon and told her not tonight because Petey was bushed and so was he. Dark Valley, he kept saying. It made him happy. But he kept her away.

Pop went up to his bedroom and went down again. Petey smelled something different. It was the Christmas after-shave. Poco something. About twenty bucks for a sniff. Petey had given it to him because the incredible-looking pale woman in the store who had red spots on her cheeks had told him to. She had smelled like she was twenty bucks a sniff also. Petey had been ready to do anything she said. So he had given Pop Poco something and Pop was wandering around the living room in a cloud of the Poco while Petey did his homework. A car crunched on the shale outside. It was a little door that slammed. Petey figured it was made in Germany by BMW. That was who it was. Miz Bean came in the door with a kind of a laugh and Petey went on doing his homework for an hour or so. It felt good hearing them downstairs. Their voices hummed in the wood of the halls and the floor. They felt like part of the house. Petey sneaked downstairs while they were talking in the living room. He didn't look. He used the john and brushed his teeth and went upstairs to bed. He finished *Hondo* again. He cried again at the part at the end where the mother and the kid are all right and Hondo stays with them. He wanted to cry but he knew how to stop it. He did.

ༀ ༀ ༀ

The year was a little crazy. It was sixty-five and then it was seventy and it was November. There was steam heat in school and everybody was sweating all the time. Everyone made jokes about armpits and showers after gym. The state cops still came and talked with Pop for two days. Volunteers who didn't know anything about libraries came and got on their hands and knees and picked things up. Miz Demeter kept telling everybody the same thing about putting books away and filing catalogue cards and consulting the shelf cards. Everybody kept doing it wrong. Pop helped and he did it wrong too. Petey volunteered but Miz Demeter wouldn't let students help because students had messed it up, she said. DiStefano stopped talking to Petey. So did Lugene. DiStefano asked her out to the roller skating party and she said maybe. Petey decided he would stop talking to Lugene. He told DiStefano he was going to cripple him. Miz Carver stopped talking to Pop. Then she started again but it was different. Miz Bean was talking to Pop for sure. Petey went to see her.

She was in her office. She was in jeans because she was helping with the library. She looked like an older kid. She looked scary that way and Petey couldn't stop looking at her. She knew that, he figured. He figured she would. She said, "Do you know what an epileptic is, Petey?"

He nodded.

"Do you know what it is when they fall down and their eyes roll back?"

"An attack," he said. "No. Wait. Seize—"

"Seizure," she said.

"That's right," Petey said.

"So," Miz Bean said, "what do you call it when five epileptic kids tear up lettuce for dinner?"

He shook his head. He knew he wasn't supposed to know.

"Seizure salad," she said. She bit her lip and laughed. Petey couldn't help laughing. He sat down on the sofa with everybody's name on it.

"That's something, the library," he said after a while.

"Somebody's angry. Somebody's in trouble," she said.

Petey said, "Somebody wants to get somebody's attention."

She nodded.

"Dumb way to do it," he said.

"*Any* way you do it, some people think," Miz Bean said. "Some people need attention really bad, or right away, or *now*. I feel sad about them. And the library. That's a shame. But did you notice? Nobody poured paint on anything, which is what happened in the Bainbridge schools last year. And nobody poured blood on the books, the way they did it in Jamesville-DeWitt. Or was it Syracuse? I don't remember. And nobody peed on the rug."

Petey couldn't help smiling for that. "They didn't write cursewords all over things either," he said.

Miz Bean said, "Maybe they can't spell. But it was pretty tame. I think it was somebody gentle who got angry at something."

Petey said, "You could swim in our pond this afternoon, it's so hot."

"I doubt I could get my bathing suit on over my jeans, Petey."

"You could change at the house, Miz Bean."

"Thank you for inviting me. That would be nice. Now maybe if the elderly person in your household invited me, I might drop over. Thank you. Are you swimming there today?"

He shrugged.

"Well," she said. "It's time to rearrange everyone's schedule again. I think I'll scramble their science classes so they can come in and spend the afternoon playing chess with me. Want to play chess?"

"Check."

She smiled like it was really funny. He smiled too. He went away happy. He usually did. But he saw Lugene and that took care of that. He saw the sweat on her lip and he felt it in his stomach. He looked at his sneakers on the stairs when she walked past him. In history when they were talking about electoral votes he punched DiStefano on the shoulder bone. Petey felt the punch up to his neck. DiStefano didn't move the whole left side of his body until after class. They chased each other around the gym until Mr. Monday came in. They went out separate doors. He wondered how much DiStefano knew about the library. Pop would find out. You could bet something on it.

49

At home there was a car waiting for them. One wheel looked square along the ground and the metal around it dragged like a crippled leg. The guy didn't have any shocks left, Petey figured. He remembered that from when Pop blew the shock absorber mount on their car. This guy's car didn't have any color left. It used to be olive but now there wasn't much of anything except silvery green and dirt. The windows looked painted over. The guy standing outside of the car was chewing tobacco and spitting it all over the shale in front of the house. He was skinny and small and he needed a shave. His shirt was ironed so hard with starch that it didn't move when the guy did. His little neck moved around inside the collar and his hairy little arms moved around under the short sleeves and it was buttoned up to the neck for a tie that wasn't there but the shirt didn't move. It just sat there while the guy moved inside it. His hair was about five inches off his head and it stayed in place with a big pompadour. It was streamlined back along the sides above the ears. The grease that held it was shiny. It wasn't grease, Petey knew. It was like with some of the corn-heads in school. Dirt did the glue job. You could smell him a ways off. He smelled like kerosene and sweat and the stink that chewing tobacco makes. His work-pants were dark blue and his shirt was light blue. You could almost see his nipples through it and the way his chest moved. But his shirt stayed still.

"I'm Reverend Staynes, S T A Y N E S. Reverend Staynes, pastor of the Faith and Beholden Tabernacle. We're down the road three miles and seven tenths from you. We're your neighbors, Mister. . . ."

Pop looked at him. He spread his legs a little and

his shoulders went back. Pop was like a dog when he
didn't like someone. You could hear the snarl, Petey
thought. It was like a low growl and only Pop and he
knew about it. Mom knew about it too. Pop never
admitted it. Petey knew it happened. So did Mom.
You could almost see the hair on his neck stand up.
Pop looked at Reverend Staynes and didn't say anything.

"We're making spaghetti and tomato sauce for the
Faith and Beholden fund raiser. We'd like to invite
you and your boy and the missus for this coming Saturday for supper and some talk."

"We don't talk about our religion," Pop said.

"Are you godless people?"

Petey figured Pop was close to putting Reverend
Staynes into his car headfirst and maybe with the door
closed.

"We're very private people," Pop said.

Reverend Staynes took his black-rimmed glasses off.
His eyes woke up. They were silvery-green. They
were the color of his car but lighter. Petey could see
them. They didn't stay still. Reverend Staynes had
this high voice but it carried. It sounded like it came
from his nose. But it went up the road from their
house and it landed on Petey. "Private is as private
does," Reverend Staynes said. "I won't ask if you won't
ask." Petey figured out what was wrong with his face.
His nose was too little for it. His head looked too big.

"Are you telling me something?" Pop shook his head
like a dog that had insects in its ears. "What the—
what *is* it? What's this? Who did you say you were?"

The little man sang it. "Reverend Joe Staynes, Faith
and Beholden Tabernacle, down the road from you

and ready to be friends. Come and eat of spaghetti with us, or stay and hold your own peace in Christ's comfort and kindness. Be of respect to us and let's us offer you the same. *Ipso facto*. It comes right around and goes back. In Latin. Here's for an afternoon of comfort, neighbors, and here's hoping it rains, on account of the wells being low."

His car wouldn't start right away. It snagged on something under the hood and just gagged. Then it started and Petey heard how the guy didn't have a muffler left. The car roared up and went away slowly. It sounded like something exploding. Pop said, "Welcome to the center of the state. Would you get the ice cubes out for me?"

Petey made a joke about that the next morning. The temperature changed by about thirty-five degrees and there was ice on the car when they left for school. Petey thought how his mom wore mittens when it was very cold. She had these fuzzy mittens somebody knitted for her. She wore a sailor's dark blue pea jacket. She looked like his big sister sometimes. When she got dressed up to go out she wore thin brown leather gloves. They were tight on the fingers. Her hands looked different and she looked like a different person. Pop would be downstairs waiting when she came up and kissed Petey goodnight before they left. Her hands were exciting in the gloves. Pop was blowing on his hands now. They were red from the cold. So were Petey's. He sat in the car with his hands in his coat pockets. He was trying to figure out whether Mom went on dates with guys who waited downstairs. He was wondering if there was anybody upstairs for her to kiss now. He was wondering if she kissed them the same and what her hands looked like in gloves now if she was wearing gloves when she kissed them good-night. Where would the house be? Who would she put upstairs? Why would she do that? He took his hands out of his pockets and blew on them. "Asshole," he said.

His father looked at him. His eyes got narrow.

"I was talking about myself," Petey said. "I'm sorry. I know."

"What?"

"Don't talk like that. Don't ever talk like that. Even if your father does."

Pop said, "Don't tell me I'm a hypocrite. You can't even spell it, much less understand it."

"H Y P O C R I T E."

"And you do know what it means."

Petey said, "I wasn't calling you that. I was calling myself that."

"Why?"

Petey just looked out the window.

They were on the dirt road. Pop said, "What did you think of the old guy yesterday? Reverend Staynes?"

"He was crazy. Anybody who preaches in a church is crazy. So's anyone who goes to it. God's crazy."

"That takes care of the history of religion," Pop said.

"God wouldn't let things be a mess like this because you wouldn't *need* God to have a mess. Everything's a mess anyway, by itself. God wouldn't need to make a mess anyway. Messes keep on happening all the time. Every day."

"You and Miss Bean have been discussing the nature of reality and everything?"

"Miz Bean. You don't say Miss anymore. It's chau-
vinist."

"Thank you."

"And we don't talk about religion."

"What do you talk about?"

"We just talk."

"About problems at home and in school and everything?"

"Pop, you want to know? Just ask me."

"Are you being fresh with me, or do you mean something?"

"Pop, I'm not a fresh kid. I sulk a lot, but I don't
badmouth you. I'm not one of those guys you have to
chain up in the guidance suite and feed him chunks of
horsemeat. Usually."

Pop laughed and wiped his nose. He blew on his
hand as he drove. Everything was gold and brown and
rust now. All the trees stood out on the hills. You could
see evergreens behind them. They were sneaking up
in front of the bare ones. Pop said, "Okay. What are
you worried about?"

"Nothing."

"You said I should just *ask*. What are you worried
about?"

"Nothing. I told you, just ask me and I'll tell you. I
told you. Everything's cool."

"Cool," Pop said. "Cool."

In the parking lot at the school Petey said, "Why do
they always cook spaghetti around here when they're
trying to raise money for Jesus?"

Pop put his arm on Petey's shoulder. Petey stayed
still. Then he moved away a little. Pop let his arm go

54

down. "Jesus was a rabbi. Being kosher, he wouldn't eat shellfish or pork."

"Thanks, Pop."

"A little father joke," Pop said.

"Thanks," Petey said. "Good luck with the library."

"Zeroing in," Pop said. "We're zeroing in on the perpetrators."

Petey looked at him but Pop was on his way to the guidance suite. Petey went to the library. There was a guy in a trooper hat blowing powder out of a squeeze bulb. Miz Demeter was watching him. Her lips were together tight. Her eyes were happy. They were also crazy. She looked like she was going to eat the trooper's hat. When she saw Petey her eyebrows lifted up. She said, "Fingerprints! We're lifting dabs on the sucker, Petey!" The trooper looked up and then he shook his head. Petey took off. In class he thought about his mother's hands in her mittens and in her gloves. He thought about the fingerprints in the library. He blew on his hands.

They chased a black man after school. They were coming out of the Great American Market with a load of pork roast and coffee and lettuce. Pop always made big salads for them. They both hated salad but it's good for you. Mom had taught him that, Petey knew. Mom had taught it to Petey too. Except Petey knew she hadn't made them eat it because it was nourishing. She loved lettuce and carrots and green peppers and rings of red onion and she had made them eat salad because it was fun for her. So they carried a pork roast and the Medaglia d'Oro coffee that Pop always used because it reminded him of what they served on

Bleecker Street and Barrow Street in New York when he was a cop at the Village precinct. Pop had the groceries on the ground and he was looking through his pockets for the keys. This old black man went to his car in a different row of the parking lot. He was wearing a sports jacket and tie and his shirt looked like he washed it a lot. His tie had a very small knot in it. It was so small that it looked tight on his neck. He was the color of the dark cherry coffee table they had in the living room. He was bald and the fringes of his hair were gray. He wore aviator sunglasses. He looked like a teacher putting bags into a square maroon Plymouth that was shiny. The old guy stood up straight. He was tall and strong looking and pretty old. With those glasses on and those clothes he looked like a teacher or an old doctor.

Pop's voice got husky. He sounded like he had a cold. He was biting his lip. He never bit his lip. He was saying, "Come on, come on, come on, come on." He was really excited. Petey got into the car and Pop said, "Seat belt."

The groceries were on the blacktop and Pop left them there. Petey said, "Pop?"

"Come on," he said. "Come on." The shiny Plymouth went out of the parking lot slowly and up the hill to the light. Pop let him go and he let a white station wagon go up and then he went up. The old guy turned toward the East River Road and Pop went after him. He kept the station wagon in between. When the wagon turned off Pop slowed down. He let a green pickup and an orange Volkswagen get ahead of him. The old guy went to King's Settlement. It was a blinking red light at a four-corners stop. The two others went straight ahead after the old guy turned right. Pop went right too and they went through the King's Settlement. It was the blinking light, the four corners, some shitboxes and trailers with white fences and a couple of big farms with real houses on them. There was an old school building made of gray wood that Pop pointed to. It was bigger than the one at Nigger Holler. People had torn old cars apart in the front yard and they'd left them there. King's Settlement Road kept climbing. There were always plenty of trailers and parts of engines and stacks of wood. Then the road leveled off in a long valley. On one side of the road there was an old red farm house with an old red barn and a lot of tractors and hoes and other machines near it. But it looked neat. It looked like somebody was keeping track of things. Across the road there was a fenced-in pasture and then a little hill in the middle of it. The hill looked like an island. On the top there was an old wall made of flat rocks. The wall was in the shape of a square. Part of the wall was crumbling. In the square but not in the middle there was a small gravestone. It looked worn out by the air rubbing against it so long. Near it but on the wall somebody had planted a little American flag on a short stick. Petey's throat hurt from looking at it all.

They drifted down off the hill and then up. He thought how he sometime would like to go and help rebuild the parts of the square wall that were falling down. Then they were climbing hard and there weren't many houses. Some of the ones they saw were falling apart. There was an uneven crossroads. There was a house on the hillside off to the left and only one wall had siding on it. There wasn't any maroon Plymouth with an old black guy in it. "Son of a bitch," Pop said.

He stuck their car's snout up one of the crossroads but then he stopped. It was like being on a horse that couldn't decide where to go. He backed up and said, "Son of a bitch" again. Then he turned them to ride back on the King's Settlement Road. They stopped at the shopping center for their groceries. They were gone. Pop said, "Son of a *bitch*," and went into the Great American and came back with two TV dinners.

All he would say to Petey on the way home was, "You don't have that many black people around here who might know something about the Holler and might be willing to tell you. What you don't do is, you don't waste them. Lose them. 'I'm a detective,'" he said. "'I find things.' That's right. I find my fingers. But only if I lose them up my—never mind." He looked at Petey. He said, "Don't grin like I'm joking with you. I'm not. I'm *pissed*."

Petey nodded. "Yes, sir," he said. He kept on grinning. He was thinking of Pop as he looked for his fingers while Petey spelled hypocrite. And he heard Pop saying to Miz Carver and her jugs, "I'm a detective. I find things." And he started to laugh.

All Pop did was shake his head. "I deserve it," he said.

Pop had his drink inside. He threw the TV dinners in the garbage. He turned the radio on and got very dark music. "Somebody knows how I feel," he said. The announcer told them it was Dvorak. Then he told them he was going to play some songs by Benjamin Britten. Petey was slicing onions. Pop was carving into a frozen loaf of bread that Miz Carver had brought over. They were laying out cheddar cheese from the little wheel covered with black wax. Pop put rings of onion on the cheese. He made six. Petey pulled the chocolate powder out for a treat and Pop said okay. Petey also pulled out a bottle of Beck's and Pop said okay again. Somebody was screaming. It was a man with a high voice singing the Benjamin Britten songs. Pop turned it off. "It sounds like what *you* listen to," he said.

"It sounded like Mom when you were having a fight."

Pop had to work on watching the cheese melt under the broiler. He had to work on opening the oven door gently and closing it partway. Petey could tell.

"After she would do that she would always say you never gave her a chance to talk. You smothered her. She said."

"You listened carefully," Pop said to the smoke coming out of the oven.

Petey turned the oven off and Pop's face got red. That was because Petey was taking over. He was acting like a grown-up. That meant Pop was a child. It might have meant disrespect. Petey didn't tell Pop he knew that. And Pop fought with it.

He said, "We must have done it a lot, and you must have listened very carefully. It must have been tough, being a kid there. At *least* tough."

Petey was putting the open sandwiches on the plates and setting out napkins and silverware. He stirred the chocolate milk and said to Pop, "Can I have a sip of your beer?"

Pop said, "Sure. Yeah. You want the whole bottle? Never mind. You're not ready. I was feeling bad about you in Brooklyn. I can't make that up to you with beer. I can't make it up. And I can't do anything at all with beer. Give me that, please." Petey pushed the beer bottle over. Pop shook his head and opened his hand. Petey slid the glass of chocolate milk over. He watched Pop sip. He made a face and sipped some more and made a face and then he took a long drink. There was a chocolate mustache on Pop's lip. Petey made himself another glass and he and Pop drank chocolate milk and ate melted cheese with onion on top. They ate all the sandwiches and Petey had two glasses of milk. Pop burped. He said, "Excuse me."

Petey said, "I'll wash up the dishes."

Pop said, "I'll dry."

Petey knew they were going to stand next to each other at the sink and tell each other something. They were going to try. They did. They couldn't, though. Pop went and turned the radio on. They listened to a program of old-time jazz. They were listening to a record of King Oliver and it was pretty good except for the record hissing over the radio and the boompity boompity sound that the tuba made. Petey was giggling about the tuba when the phone rang.

He jumped for it and Pop turned the radio off. The hissing while nobody talked over the telephone sounded like the hissing of the jazz record. Then a man said, "Colored is the curse God laid upon the race." There was the hiss. Then there was, "You hear?" Then there was a sound like a cork coming out of a bottle and Petey was alone on the line.

While he was still holding onto the telephone he said, "Colored—God cursed the race? It was some weirdo. Colored something something race. God cursed something."

"A crank call?"

"It sho was not mah bookie makin' *good*," Petey said. He thought he sounded like Kingfish on an Amos 'n Andy tape.

"Don't talk like that," Pop said.

"Sorry."

"Some crank called and told you something about colored people?"

"I guess so."

"They're a curse on somebody? That's the general idea? It was a bigot telling you something bad about blacks?"

"He sounded like he knew," Petey said. "He sounded like a full-time professional at saying things about people."

"You get me on if he calls again. You listen if he calls when you're alone. You write down what he says, then you hang up. Then you get me. You lock the door and you get me. When you go out—I don't know. Be careful. That helps a lot, doesn't it?"

"*Use your head* is what you usually say."

"Do it."

"I will."

When Miz Bean came over later on Petey was upstairs doing homework. The book gave them a chapter to read and a mimeographed crossword puzzle that asked questions about the chapter. Petey wanted to tell somebody that if the book wanted to know something it should just ask and not horse around with games. He was going to go and tell Pop. He stopped because it was just what Pop would have said. They were getting to sound like each other, Petey thought. That wasn't healthy. Or maybe it was. Living mostly alone together was tough on them. Sometimes it was terrible. Maybe they should do something. Petey couldn't figure out what. Maybe they should do something like go out and get a dog or a gerbil or a parrot. He heard Miz Bean come in and he decided he should tell her about the problem of living together alone too much. He wondered if she would think it was a problem. Many varieties of what he knew as bullshit in his life she always ended up describing as *healthy*. Petey decided he was getting tired of that too. If you know something's a total pain in the ass it can be very tiring when somebody tells you that it's really good for you. He would have to watch himself. He was getting tired of too much. That's when you dope up. That's when you booze up and crash in some cornhead's car. He thought of the old man in the maroon Plymouth and he wondered why Pop was doing all this seeking and searching and trailing. That was when he wondered if maybe Pop was getting tired of things too. Maybe Pop was getting tired of him.

Miz Bean's voice came up through the grate. He heard glass on glass and a gurgle. That meant that Pop was pouring out white wine for Miz Bean. Petey sat with his back against the wall near the heat grate. He heard them better that way. He liked being upstairs and going to sleep while they talked. It sounded like a house then. He got into bed. He got out and went downstairs. He was sneaky and fast in his bare feet. He peed and brushed his teeth and rubbed at the grease around his nose with soap. He reminded himself to get up early and take a shower before school. He sneaked upstairs and got into bed with the lights out. He hung his head off the bed to listen. But then he laid it right on the edge of the pillow. Pop's voice was deep and rough and terrific because it sounded sure about everything. Miz Bean's was pretty deep too. They both sounded like they were in the wood that the house was made of. Everything was part of that. They were all part of the voices humming in the wood.

"We would call it obsessional, nearly," Miz Bean said. "In some kind of clinical conference, if they were talking about you and your abiding interest in pockets of Negro life in America where Negroes don't live, you would be referred to as obsessive. Is that why you're doing it? Because you can metaphorically look into an absence? Are you dealing with absent things by dealing with *other* absent things? Because if that's so, then you've got problems. You're looking for something you can't find. Which could mean that you don't want to find the *other* thing—which you're *really* looking for. You know?"

Pop said, "Everybody always has to deal with absent things. The rest of it's hoo-hah. With all due respect. I enjoy inquiring. That's all."

"Maybe. Maybe. But then I can't figure out why you *quit* inquiring. Professionally, I mean."

"Sometimes you feel like it's time. You have to stop clean and get out and start clean. That's all. That's all of it. That's all there is to it, Lizzie. And of course I had to leave. You know that."

"All right," she said. "How's Pete doing?"

"You know him. He's tense. He's locked up tight.

63

He is not the most reachable kid I ever saw. I mean—he's terrific, though, right? He's decent and pretty polite. Did you see the wall he made near the barn? The kid can build. He's—he sees things. I don't know how to describe it. I think what happens is, he gets this vision of something in his mind. He gets an idea about something and he sees all of it right away. The first time. Complete. Understand? Entirely whole. He saw the whole wall. I'm sure of it. He's terrifically talented. If we ever figure it out—if *he* does, if he figures it out, what to do with his talent. Whatever it's for."

"Oh, he will," Miz Bean said. "You'll back him up, and some teacher will discover him, and he'll be a certified genius someplace."

"I'd settle right now for a B-minus average and we bribe his way into some ag and tech."

"You don't mean that."

"He's eccentric, Lizzie. The world isn't easy on eccentrics."

"He'll run the world for the normals. Don't worry. I'd rather have Petey for a kid than all those middle-class pimples who go around acting like fledgling golf pros. You stick with Petey."

"Thank you, mother. I will."

"What'd you call me?"

"What? Mother? That was bad?"

"Nope."

"You're all right?"

"I'm terrific. But I don't live at Nigger Holler. So how come you're sniffing around it so much? Unless Bernice Carver has set up a tent or a trailer down there?"

"Oh, don't Bernice Carver me. I wasn't the one

seeking an open and honest whatchamacallit with you know who."

"Don't call him any names, okay? He was my prof. I really respect him. He made a couple of mistakes about me and him, and people do that all the time. Okay? Maybe I did too."

"I apologize."

"No, you're courteous, and you don't usually have much to apologize for. Petey gets it from you. You're a nice, polite, tough cop, and he's as nice as his father. You're both sometimes even courtly, actually. Petey more than you because he's classier. But you're both pretty good people."

Petey was smiling so hard in the dark that he thought the skin at the corners of his mouth might be splitting. He thought about the blood that would be on his pillow if his face tore like that and then he couldn't get back to the good feelings Miz Bean had given him in the darkness. He thought about the guy who talked on the phone about God's curse. He remembered Pop's face when he described the call to him. He thought about Miz Bean downstairs with Pop. It was awfully quiet. It was as quiet as one of these roads going past shitboxes and shacks in the middle of the night when all the windows were dark and the TVs were off and there was just the wind. It was like Nigger Holler. For a second Petey thought he knew why Pop would get interested in Nigger Holler. Because a new secret is better than what you know if what you know hurts you and doesn't do you any more good than it did the first time you knew that you knew it. If he could remember this he was going to ask Miz Bean if she thought that was true about Pop. Maybe though he still really *was* a detective. That was the other thought. Maybe Pop was on an undercover assignment and the perpetrators were in Nigger Holler or something like that. Maybe they were black perpetrators. He thought of the trooper looking for fingerprints. There was no more talking downstairs. He thought about the rubber bulb as the trooper squeezed it. The white powder puffed out. Squeeze and squeeze and squeeze.

He heard the door close and the lock snap and Miz Bean's BMW try to start a couple of times. It was cold and it was very late. As soon as he had wakened he'd been able to feel the lateness. When she drove away he could see her lights on the road and the roadside. All the trees looked connected near the top by their bare branches. In the light from her car the branches looked cold and scaly. They looked like lizards' tails locked together while the lizards slept. Then the lights were gone and everything was shiny black. He heard the wind move but he couldn't see any motion. Pop was walking around the house. His footsteps went into the living room but he didn't stay there long. Petey figured this might be an all-nighter. Pop would go from room to room. When Petey came down in the morning Pop would be standing next to the stove with his eyes red.

Petey went downstairs. He put his bathrobe on first and then his fur-lined slippers so that Pop wouldn't have an excuse to send him back up or holler at him. It was like Pop had been expecting him. There was a fire going in the wood stove and there was tea in the tall white china mugs. He sat and watched Petey spoon the sugar in.

66

Petey said, "You knew I was coming down, huh?"

"I heard you. Since when do kids have trouble sleeping?"

"Sometimes they do."

"You do?"

"Sometimes."

"A lot?"

"Sometimes," Petey said. "How about you?"

"You know me," Pop said. "I'm the original Wandering Jew. You know that story?"

Petey shook his head.

Pop said, "Do you want to?"

Petey lifted his shoulders and dropped them.

"Another time," Pop said. "You could look it up or something. Mrs. Demeter must have something on it."

"Miz Demeter."

"Excuse me." Then he said, "Listen to that." There was the stove ticking. It did that when it got hot and when it cooled off. There was wind and the sound of heat going up the stovepipe. There was the sound of something far away going farther. "It's a jet. Listen to it. I think it's one of the big ones. You believe that? Three o'clock in the morning and a couple of guys like us are down here with a pot of tea, and there's a plane up there, five miles up and how far away? And people are drinking drinks and eating steak and going to someplace exciting. How'd you like—"

"It's a military jet, Pop. I think it's Strategic Air Command from Griffiss. That's in Rome, that's about sixty, seventy miles from here? It's a bomber and it's probably filled with guys smoking cigars and drinking beer."

"They wouldn't drink beer on duty, would they?"

"In a movie they did. It looked pretty true."

"Oh," Pop said. "Well. And here I was, being romantic. And here you are, dumping all over me."

"I'm not dumping, Pop. I didn't come down here for that."

"No," Pop said. "No. You wanted to keep me company and here *I* am, dumping. Huh?"

Petey looked into his tea. It was exactly the color of the skin of the old man in the maroon Plymouth who got away from them. "Nobody's dumping," Petey said.

His father said, "Are you miserable, Pete? Are you ready to die, you're so unhappy?"

Petey watched the tears that came off his face and fell into the tea. He hated crying like that. He knew how to stop it. He did. It almost didn't work but then it did. Then it didn't again. Pop was standing next to him and hugging his head and neck and shoulders against his waist and hip bone and the bottom of his heavy belly. He stood there and held Petey tight and Petey sat straight most of the time. He did lean in. But mostly he sat straight.

Pop said, "Could you talk to me? Could you tell me something about it, Pete? Is it school? Or Mom? Or how I hang around with Lizzie Bean? Or do I mess around with the ladies too much in general? Is it school?"

"I gotta go to bed, Pop."

His father hugged again and let him go. He sat back down at his place at the table and leaned down to his tea as he lifted the cup up and drank some. But his eyes were on Petey when he tilted the cup. Petey looked back at him. He wasn't crying. He wiped his nose and sniffed and stopped.

"Jesus, Petey. Don't wipe your nose on your sleeve. Your mother got the robe from *Brooks* Brothers."

"It itches."

"Yeah. She gave me one too, several years ago. Mine's blue, though. With the red piping on the pockets? Remember it?" Petey shrugged. "Why should you? But I've still got it upstairs. I couldn't wear it a lot because it itched so much."

"I don't mind wearing it," Petey said. "She gave it to me for my birthday. Or Christmas maybe. I forget."

The telephone rang. "Don't answer it," Pop said. "I'll get it." He went to the wall near the kitchen door but by the time he had his hand on it the telephone had stopped ringing. Pop looked at the phone. Petey thought he might pull it off the wall and beat it against the cupboards.

"That's—you think that's him? The one with Jesus' curse?"

"I thought you told me it was God's curse."

"Yeah. He said it was God's curse."

"Okay. We have to get it right. If it happens again, we have to get it right." Pop's face was red. He looked like his heart was blamming away. Squeeze and squeeze and squeeze. Pop said, "Don't worry."

Petey said, "Not me, man."

"Cool, man," Pop said. He sounded dumb. He was trying to sound funny and he ended up dumb. Petey didn't think it was entirely fair for his father. Pop said, "Don't worry. Go to bed. I'm here."

Petey stood on the steps and listened to his father's

heavy walking. He followed the sound of it with his ears. He heard Pop's feet in the pantry. He heard the lid of the big pot. He even thought he could hear the soft gray cloth. When Pop released the drum Petey could hear the softest click. He thought of Pop with the revolver in his hand. He thought of himself. Squeeze.

THE FOREST WAS downhill from their house and back from the road. There was a rotted old garden that Pop had said he would till and plant and harvest. He wouldn't. There was a falling-down fence and inside of it there were rotten tomato plants lying on the ground. Old corn stalks were eaten by animals at night. Petey's window looked out over the garden and the turning in the road. At night he could hear them. He heard little footsteps. Something was being careful. He heard tearing sounds and breaking and jaws. The wind was rattling the dead plants. So was something else. Even in the winter you would hear things in the snow, he figured.

Down from the dead garden was the forest. The hillside was steep and the dirt was all mixed with clay and it got slippery. Petey had cut a trail through it. He got permission to use the axe and some old garden shears. He cut bushes with thorns and berries on them and he cut small trees. He sometimes piled stones to mark the way. Sometimes he piled stones to fill small valleys so somebody would be able to walk through more easily. Pop had never walked up to the top of their land. This was so he could walk to the bottom. In the springtime when he was done he would get Pop to take his drink along and they could walk down the hills and turns and over the log bridge he was building. The end of Petey's trail was at the end of their property. There were more trees and rocks and bugs and deer droppings but that wasn't their land. Past the iron pipe some surveyor had driven into the ground wasn't their land. They could stand there and Pop could drink his drink and they could look things over. They would know what belonged to them.

It was getting to be the end of November and school was getting to be a total bitch. There wasn't any word on the library trashing and Pop wouldn't talk about it anymore. He said it was pending. Pending. Like in the cop movies. Pending. And they changed their shops. He was in wood shop now. He liked winding steel wool around a drill press bit while it was spinning. That was how he would smooth down the inside of a wooden napkin ring he had made. He did that four times. He thought they ought to buy some cloth napkins to go with them. Pop said one of these days they would. And they moved them out of music. He was grateful. You can get very tired of singing, "Oh my *darl*ing Clem-en-*tine*." You can get very tired of this complete hippo with braces on her teeth at forty-five years old at least who bangs with her fat fingers on the piano and makes you *sing*. "Sometimes I live in the country," they had to sing. "Sometimes I live in the town." Then she would look at them so they would get the idea that this was *very* meaningful stuff. They would all have to point their chins up at the ceiling and wail out, "Some*times* I take a great *no*-shun," and then she would get completely cross-eyed with dying for love or something else and she would lead them. "Jump *in*-to the *riv*-uh and *drown*." Sure. But what they did like was that a famous black killer sang that song and conned his way into a pardon. "And all for *mus*ic," she would say. Then somebody would do an intentional fart and that would be that.

They moved them out of music into art. The teacher was Mr. Van Camp. He was as big as Pop. He dressed preppy and he wore bow ties. He smiled a lot. He pushed his glasses up onto his nose a lot. When a kid named Green tried walking out of his class because he was making them cut up colored paper and paste it onto other colored paper, Mr. Van Camp got up from his chair and stood in front of Green. Green gave him the finger, the cross-armed Fuck You, the hand-under-armpit-squeezed fake fart, and a lot of big lip. Mr. Van Camp shoved him in the shoulder but up near the front of his chest. Green fell back three steps and said, "*Ow*." But he came back. Mr. Van Camp made a fist like a hammer and brought it down on top of Green's head. Green fell down crying. Mr. Van Camp was shaking a little but he came back to the front of the room and told them to paste. Green went back to his seat. After a few days he had them copying things. Petey was copying out an entire medieval castle. After two sessions of that he stopped copying and started making it up. He was drawing every rock in the outside wall. He did it on Mondays and Thursdays and they were good times of the week. Mr. Van Camp watched him do it and smiled. Petey didn't mind smiling back.

The rest of his schedule was the same. Lugene was the same. So was Pop. In history Miz Carver was nice but she wasn't all that pleased with him anymore. He could tell by the way she looked at him to be certain he knew. Whoever made the weird phone call let it ring once and hung up on Pop. But that was all. No one bothered them. The Reverend Staynes didn't come around. They chased the wrong black guy once. He drove away from the Holler in the direction of Binghamton and Pop got disgusted. He looked at his maps but he wasn't as excited anymore. Miz Bean was the same. They were sitting around in her office. She was behind her desk. She was wearing new perfume. Petey thought there was some kind of berry smell in it. She was wearing a fuzzy sweater with sleeves that ended exactly where her hands began. Her hands looked very big and strong while she wrote things. Kids were coming in to get things signed and bitch about their teachers. People kept calling her up and her hair kept falling in front of her eyes when she bent down to the telephone. The rest of her hair was short and it stopped under her ears. On her forehead it went almost to her eyes. She looked like she was trying to figure out how to move closer to the people who were talking on the phone. Her voice was low. When she laughed it was lower. He sat on the sofa with all the names on it and he leaned his head back and closed his eyes. It sounded like her voice at night sometimes when she and Pop were talking and then her car door slammed and she would drive away very late.

He opened his eyes. She was almost whispering. Then she was just nodding her head. He could see how filled up her eyes were. She was nodding again. She said, "Wonderful." Then she said, "Congratulations. You're all so lucky. I'm so happy for all of you." She nodded again and she hung up the phone.

Without looking she said, "Petey, close the door."

He did. He sat down to wait.

She said, "That was somebody I went to graduate school with quite a few years ago. She's an old lady. She's as old as I am."

"You're thirty-four," Petey said.

"What else do you hear around the house?"

"None of that stuff," Petey said.

"What stuff? None of *what?*"

"You know. Making out and everything."

"Adults don't make out, Petey."

"I'm not saying that they do, Miz Bean."

She said, "Don't." Then she said, "I'm thirty-five. I had a birthday last week. That was when your father and I went out for a dreadful dinner that you didn't want to come to."

"There was a flick on the tube."

"You wanted to be nice to us, I think. Anyway, I told this to your father. I'll tell it to you. On the phone just now, that was a woman who was a girl with me. We were pretty good friends. She got married and she had this baby. It was born dead. Can you imagine that?"

"Bad genes," Petey said.

Her eyes were still wet but her face loosened up. "You ever hear the saying about a little knowledge?"

"Pop says it wouldn't hurt me to get hold of some."

"Different saying. All right. Genes, whatever. The baby was stillborn. That's what they call it. And something happened to her organs."

"Uterus," Petey said. "Womb. Ovaries. Tubes. Some kind of tubes."

"So they decided they'd adopt a baby because trying to have one the other way could kill her. So they did it. That's what she called about."

Petey said, "Yeah?"

"Isn't it beautiful?" Miz Bean said. This time one of the tears got out. He watched it. Then he looked someplace else. He heard her blow her nose. He looked again. Her face looked chapped all of a sudden. She said, "You tell me things."

Petey nodded.

She said, "You tell me all kinds of things all the time."

He said, "I wouldn't repeat what you told me. Is that what you mean? Anyway, who'd I tell?"

"This is about me," Miz Bean said. "I'm giving it to you and you can do whatever you think you should with it. I'd just as soon you just held onto it for me. Your father knows all about it now. Your father and I are good friends. We're excellent friends. And you can have this too." She blew her nose again and said, "When I was a good deal younger I got pregnant. I had a baby. A doctor who was a friend of mine helped me have this baby. I couldn't take care of it. I was a little crazy. You know how it goes, times like that."

Petey nodded. He said, "You got it adopted?"

She said, "I did. What do you think."

"Good deal," Petey said. "Smart move." He looked

at her. He looked at her and then he sat up. He said, "Miz Bean? Am I your kid?"

"Oh," she said. "Oh, darling Pete. Oh. Sweetheart, wouldn't that be perfect for us?" She was crying now. She said, "No. No. I'm sorry, but no."

He said, "Should we check it? Is there a way we could check on it?"

She blew her nose. It was red. She said, "No, darling."

"You're sure, huh?"

"I'm afraid I am, Petey."

"Yeah," he said.

"I'm sorry."

"Yeah."

"You know about me now," she said. "You know something about me now."

Petey stood up. He said, "I have to go to class."

"Then open the door," Miz Bean told him. "Make your escape."

It was cold that afternoon. It was getting dark and it was cold and there was rain all through the air. It almost didn't fall. It almost hung there. It was like being in a very cold cloud. He was working on the trail. He was clearing roots that kept springing back from the axe. He wasn't doing well. Somebody was shooting something and he kept on hearing the noise. But he wasn't thinking about noises. He was remembering his mother at home.

He was also trying to figure out why so many of the cornheads hadn't been to school. He was wondering why he didn't pay attention to things. There were reasons for a lot of things but not for everything. But there were enough reasons to make sense of a little of what went on. The trouble was he didn't watch hard enough, he decided. He was hacking at roots and the hard slippery branches of tough bushes and the axe kept whisking near his work shoes. That was enough to pay attention to. And there was plenty else. But a lot of the cornheads weren't in class. The school felt like a castle when fewer people walked down the halls. They felt longer and wider. He felt like he was on patrol. He would carry a long wide sword that took two hands to hack with. He thought of the castle he was drawing in art class.

He thought of the day his mother took him to the Museum of Natural History. They rode the BMT over the bridge and he looked down at the East River. He always did. He always imagined what it would look like if the bridge caved in and the train slid down the torn tracks into the water. In Manhattan they took another train and rode through tunnels. In the museum it was early and nobody was there except guards. They were old and they looked sleepy. He and his mother checked their coats at a counter in the lobby. Everything smelled from some kind of oil. It went with the building. The ceilings looked a hundred feet high. Everything was stone and shiny and everything looked like it weighed thousands of pounds. His mom said she kept getting lost because she hadn't been there for such a long time. He wondered if she ever had been there because she got lost so much. The night before his parents had been fighting about being an ignorant person and never learning about finer things and culture. His mother had said how many times she used to go to the Museum of Natural History and other museums before they got married. His father had said, "Bullshit."

His mother had said, "You have the manners to go with your education. You sound like a guttersnipe."

His father had laughed. He had said, "Guttersnipe? They don't *say* guttersnipe anymore. Gutter—you know, I really love you."

His mother had said, "I'll consider it. I'll take it under advisement. But *really. . . .*"

In the morning she had gotten him up and told him to dress up in his good corduroys and a shirt and sweater because they were going to the Museum of Natural History.

There were tremendous canoes with dummies in them. They carried spears and blow guns that made him think of pea shooter season in the spring. Everybody bought plastic tubes and bags of dried peas and they would go around spitting the peas at each other. One room was dark and long. There were rows and rows of totem poles. They looked like the faces of vicious dogs. Some of them looked frightened or very sick. But most of them looked angry at everything. There wasn't any noise in that room. When someone's shoe scraped, his stomach felt like a balloon being blown up.

Another room was smaller and even darker. Records of drums and flutes kept playing over and over. There were models of people in boats and people living in huts and people cooking. There were tools and weapons all over. He was trying to figure out how some of the fire-starting equipment worked when the songs they were playing got inside his head. All of a sudden he heard them. All of a sudden he listened to them. They were very slow and very sad. They were moaning. It was like someone who was very, very sick and saying so. It was like dying. He was listening to somebody die. The record stopped. He figured that the man was dead. There was quiet for a few seconds. Then another song started. It sounded like the same man. It was like listening to a ghost.

His mom found him in the lobby. She didn't shout at him for taking off. She didn't ask him what the matter was. She told him to stay there and she got their coats and they left. She kept her hand on his arm all the way down the steps. When they were at the curb she whistled for a cab. Petey always smiled when she did that. She could whistle between her teeth and his father couldn't and Pop could never help noticing it. They rode downtown until they got to a huge movie theater. They went inside without talking and they watched *The Empire Strikes Back*. He loved it. He loved the way Han Solo got turned into a block of metal. He hated it for Han and Princess Leah. But he loved the way that worked. They ate candy and popcorn. Darth Vadar tried to kill his son. He didn't want to but he had to. The details were so beautiful. The stars and the parts of the ships and the floating city were so beautiful.

Outside his mother said, "You see what I mean about culture?"

"What?"

"Exactly what I say," she said.

He was remembering that. He was bent over and working on his trail. Suddenly he straightened up to get ready. He heard something. "What?" he called. He saw Pop. "What?"

But Pop was carrying him up and along the trail and then off it. He stopped and put him down. He grabbed his sleeve and pulled him along. "Jesus," Pop said. He was panting. "Don't you pay attention to anything? Listen!" Petey heard the guns going off.

He said, "Hunters?"

"It's the first goddamned day of deer season is all," Pop said. His face was red and he was talking with his teeth together. Petey knew he was in trouble. "It's the late afternoon of the day when all the drunk fools and trigger-happy teenagers cutting school and senile white hunters are out here because you happen to live in prime deer country. They're all shooting each other and whatever trees are between them. I mean, they're killing children in yellow raincoats on tricycles, for Christ's sake, because they're positive that they are really deer in disguise. So that would be what the matter is. See where you were? Look at where you were down there. What can you see? What would a hunter see? A good hunter, much less the lost battalions we've got wandering around here."

"Nothing," Petey said.

Pop took a deep breath. "Worse than nothing. They could see your shape. Something dark, moving in the brush. Blam!"

Petey flinched.

Pop saw that. He took another deep breath. He put his hand on top of Petey's head and he smiled. Petey saw that he made himself smile. "Don't want to get shot up, right?"

Petey looked at him. He kept looking. He remembered to say, "No, sir."

"Come up to the house. Let's get red hats on when we go outside. One of those knitted red hats. Would you stay out of the woods for a while?"

Petey was thinking of him and Pop at the last part of the trail. They would be looking into the woods. Pop would have his drink in his hand and it would be spring. Petey said, "Could I just wear the red hat and keep on working on my trail?"

More shots went off. Pop looked up. The shots went again and Pop said, "Come on."

They walked uphill. They came out of the woods near the house and walked up to the road. They followed it past the house. Coming down the field across from the house and toward the barn were two men dragging a dead deer. Pop walked faster. The men saw him coming and stopped. They were going under the old fence. They held the sagging barbed wire up for each other. They looked at Pop and they talked to each other. Pop slowed down. He walked like a cop now. Petey stayed a little behind him.

"Hello," Pop said.

One of the men was big. He had a mustache and big ears and a bright face. He kept smoking a cigarette. He was dressed in army clothes and high boots. He wore his rifle over his shoulder. It had a telescopic sight on it. The other man was short and he had a mechanical left arm. It went in two rods from the elbow down to a hook. He was holding the barbed wire with his hook. The big man smiled and said, "Hi." The little man pointed with his hook at the deer. It was very small. Petey wondered if it was a fawn.

Pop said, "I didn't post my land because people around here told me that hunters would ask if they could cross on it."

"You're right," the big man said. "We should have asked. Do you mind if we finish dragging through? There's a car coming around to meet us."

There was a shot above them. Everybody ducked and then looked up. A man in an orange suit showed at the woods at the top of their hill and then went back in when he saw them. "Assholes," Pop said. "All these guys who don't know what in hell they're doing. Do you guys know what you're doing?"

"Take a look," the big man said. His voice was high.

Pop looked down at the deer. He looked in close. Petey could see him pretending to study it. "What is it—golden retriever, or some kind of mixed breed?" Pop asked. "Or—you mean that's your deer? Oh. Well. Sure. You guys put that little deer in the glove compartment of your car and don't hunt here any-more. Okay? Tell your friends. Please don't hunt here."

Pop was looking up the hill into the big man's eyes and Petey felt bad about being embarrassed because of his father. He knew he shouldn't be at a time like this. The big man looked down at Pop. They were pretty close to each other. Petey thought he could smell the deer's skin or its blood. Petey saw Pop spread his legs a little. He watched the toes of Pop's shoes to see if he was bouncing up to move after the big man. But the shoes stayed still and so did Pop. The big man licked his lip. They kept looking at each other. Then the man with the hook said, "No problem, right?"

Pop looked up at the big man. When the big man said, "Nope," Pop gave them half a little salute and turned around. He walked past Petey but put his hand back. Petey didn't know what he wanted. He moved his fingers a few times. Petey took his hand. Pop pulled him along to the house. He was gentle and happy. Inside he made a big drink. He blew air out and out again. Petey hung around with him for a while. They talked about things. Pop said he'd make their dinner alone. Petey went upstairs to his room to work on the drawing of the castle. He wanted to finish the third row of stones. He wanted to get them lined up right and draw each one perfectly.

That night Pop drifted a lot. Petey fell asleep and woke up again to hear Pop on the stairs or on the downstairs sofa or in the kitchen making tea. When he woke up another time he knew it was late because the darkness felt solid and heavy. Pop was snoring downstairs. Petey put a sweatshirt and dungarees on and then downstairs he put boots on over his bare feet. They were Pop's mud boots. They felt wet and cold. He thought of someone wearing someone else's skin. He plopped as softly as he could out the door with a flashlight in his hand. He went off the porch and down. He went down to his trail and then along it. Everything looked larger or smaller than it was supposed to be. Branches and the trunks of trees and stalks in the dead garden looked different. Things rattled at him. Then he was through the garden and below it. He fell because of the boots but all he did was bang himself. He came to his half-finished bridge. In the darkness he was frightened. He said it to himself the way he thought he would tell one of the cornheads

86

or DiStefano the townie. He said, "Man, I was scared to shit. I mean, I was *scared*." He was at his bridge but he was afraid to shine the light over to the other side. That was where the trail went on a couple of dozen feet and petered out to nothing. That was where his fort would be. That was where their land ended and where the darker forest began. He didn't want to look there. Suddenly he didn't want to look anywhere. He found the axe and picked it up and said, *"There."* He needed to make the noise. Then he went back up.

His face felt cold because of the air. His feet felt cold because the boots were like someone else's skin. His neck felt cold because he was frightened in the darkness where everything was bigger or smaller than he was used to. But his face felt cold because the temperature was falling and because there was wetness in the air. Pop had said it would snow soon and the deer hunters would be happy because they could follow footprints. That was after they had finished the pork chops and Pop was leaning back. He was thinking of the men he had chased. Petey knew that because he was also thinking about them and mostly how tough Pop had been and how scared Petey had been and also how embarrassed. He wished he wouldn't feel embarrassed because of Pop. He felt embarrassed because of everything. A lot of his life was possibly Pop's and his mother's fault. So why not get pissed off at the old man? Petey was feeling better and Pop was feeling good and then Pop said it would snow for the hunters and then he laughed. "They couldn't follow tracks anyway," Pop had said. "They'll walk in circles with the tracks or without them. They get mad enough, they'll put a couple of rounds into the garage or something, the ass end of the garage maybe. Then they'll go back and get drunker to stay warm, they'll shoot somebody's toes off. I saw somebody get their toes shot off one time. A doughty officer running with his piece drawn and pointing it down. One stumble, and one small fall, and ka-boom: compensatory pay for life. The dumb die last."

Now Petey went across the road very quickly. He had halfway run across the lawn once he had come up through the dead garden. He was too scared to slow down. But he didn't want to go inside. He wanted to cross the road and go up. He held the axe with the blade out so he wouldn't fall on it. He went under the fence and up the hard hill. It was getting colder fast and the winds were beginning to blow around their house. When you were in bed upstairs you could hear them coming around the corner of the chimney and the roof of the garage. They made whistling noises and it felt good to be sleeping cold and under a lot of blankets that still smelled from the mothballs in Brooklyn. Pop had said he thought these were all new blankets but Petey was pretty sure that one or two came from the house in Brooklyn because they smelled from the wood chest filled with mothballs that his parents had always kept at the foot of their bed.

He stood still at the top until he caught his breath. Once he stopped hearing himself he listened to everything else. There wasn't anybody or anything around him or near him or near the house. He heard the wind and he heard the dead stalks all the way down in the garden. He heard little things in bushes below him but he knew they were small animals and maybe some wild hunting cat. He stood holding the axe across his body with his hands hanging full length and his head up to listen. He looked along the ridge. It was really a ridge more than a hill. It ran along their road and after a mile or two when their road went north toward towns the ridge kept going. It ended near a little valley with some ponds and a marsh and a house that was never painted and never fixed up or changed but always had smoke coming from the chimney. The man inside was always making things out of metal and plastic and cloth. He welded small girders and rods to make shapes. Pop called them geodesic. There was a well with a geodesic roof shape over it. The well had letters on it made of shiny metal. They said DON'T TREAD ON ME. There were heaps of firewood and a lot of garden in the front and back. The man looked out of his window sometimes, but never for very long.

Petey wondered why he was standing up on his hill and thinking about a guy who had all these weird-ass shapes around his house. He tried to think about himself. He couldn't feel anything important. He decided finally to think about Lugene. He couldn't remember her face. He remembered her breath. It smelled sweet because it smelled of bubble gum. She thought he was immature. He wasn't allowed to hang around town. He wasn't allowed to go to the roller skating place because his father said bums came there to sell the kids beer and marijuana and pills. He also said it didn't have enough exits and it was a firetrap. He wasn't allowed to see R-rated movies. He didn't have cool boots. He wore the trash felt-lined Canadian boots his father had bought him. He didn't have a hatchet so he could work on his trail and his bridge. He'd have to use the axe and he'd probably chop his toes off. "The dumb die last," his father had said. Well maybe. The stars were going out. There hadn't been much moon to start with and now the stars were going out. He'd been standing there and while he looked the stars had started disappearing and he suddenly had known it. Then he understood that it meant clouds that would carry in the snow. He started to shiver all of a sudden. He was cold and he felt damp all the way through his skin. He felt miserable the way he did when he caught a flu. He wished that he would stop wishing for his mother. He didn't want to be a child all his life. He also knew that you were a child as long as you had a parent. What he wondered was how you knew when you had them. He went down the hill. He left the axe on the porch near some wood he had stacked so they could get to it in case of a blizzard. He went in and up to bed. Pop said, "What?" Petey figured he was dreaming. He began to fall asleep right away. He wondered what would happen if they both dreamed at once about the same thing. He wondered if they'd meet.

There was snow that morning and more snow in the afternoon. Everybody acted like they'd never seen snow. They looked out windows. They opened windows to scrape snow off the ledges to throw snowballs across the classroom at each other. DiStefano made an ice ball and dropped it down the back of Lugene's blouse when they were walking on the stairs. Petey smiled when she screamed. But he knew Lugene and DiStefano were feeling things about that ice ball that he wasn't. He knew it was because he didn't have an ice ball. He knew it was because he didn't have any balls at all. He smiled about his joke but he wasn't happy about it. The heat was on full bore. The school smelled like hot water and creamed corn. It tasted like glue. DiStefano and a couple of guys ran a contest to see who could hold a bowl of creamed corn upside down the longest. A guy named Bister won. They always called him Blister. So DiStefano went around collecting a nickel from everybody in the contest to give to the Blister of Bowel. That was how DiStefano pronounced it. Petey gave a nickel even though he wasn't in the contest. He wanted to be. Then Bister showed everybody the deck of cards. The back of every card showed people doing it in a different position. Petey was afraid to look. Then he wanted to see more. Bister wouldn't show him. "Everybody *stand!*" Bister called. The guys at the table looked at each other and started to laugh. Nobody could stand because everybody had a rod on account of the pictures. Petey saw Pop coming over and he wanted to take off. He couldn't stand, though. So he sat there and leaned back. He knew he looked like a smartass and he knew Pop would think he wanted to act like one. But he couldn't stand up. Pop walked past them. He didn't look. Petey watched him go. "Everybody *stand!*" Bister called again. Petey could and he did. He took off.

He saw Miz Bean upstairs. He was going to sit in her office and talk to her. He was hoping she would hug him. He knew that. He didn't know why. He didn't know if it was because of the pictures or because Pop walked past him that way. He smiled his big smile at her. She raised her eyebrows and waved. Then she looked back down at her desk. He looked at her legs as he walked past her. He saw her see him do it. He felt like a total jerk. In art he worked on the fort. He kept wishing he could work on a real one. He also wished he could hang around the roller skating barn. Cornheads always called any big building a barn. But he did wish he could just stand around there and not feel like a jerk. He did every rock perfectly and he made each one so small he had to lean over the paper and nearly touch his face to it. He wondered if he would ruin his eyes and need glasses. All he had to do was get big glasses and some pimples around his mouth and on his forehead to qualify for Dingleberry of the Eighth Grade award. He started another rock.

He didn't want to go to the library that day. He had to because Miz Carver gave them research projects and she was being tough on him. It wasn't fair but it was because of Pop so it made a little sense. Anything that made sense was better than something that didn't. He went to the library. He had to look up stuff about Teddy Roosevelt. He looked at the shelves but not at the card catalogue. It took longer that way but he did it that way. He found some books and carried them over to a table near the windows. Someone had written in heavy letters on the table LIFE SUCKS. Petey got his pen out to carry on the conversation. He couldn't think of anything to say. He looked at the pictures in one of the books and then he started to read it. He didn't care. He looked in the *Encyclopedia Americana* because it sometimes sounded like baby-talk. He was in the mood for that. Except it told him that Theodore Roosevelt had founded the Museum of Natural History in the city of New York. Bully. So he was thinking about his mother and then the time she took him there. He didn't want to think about that. He stopped himself pretty well. He thought about the time he went up on the roof of an apartment house on Avenue I and Ocean Avenue with a pocketful of rocks. He threw one out into the middle of Ocean Avenue when the traffic had stopped for a light. He landed it in a convertible. The guy looked right up and saw him. Petey watched the guy pull up on his parking brake and leave the car in the middle of traffic and come tearing over to the building and then out of sight. He was heading for the lobby, Petey figured. He was coming for him. Petey got off over the roof of the building that was connected to the one he was on. He went down the stairs. The guy came after him. He was an old guy with no hair but he ran fast and he looked like he wanted to kill Petey. It was on his face like a sign: GONNA GET YOUR ASS. Petey ran down to the Cut. It went behind all the two-family houses and apartment houses alongside the Long Island Railroad tracks that were downhill from the bushes that grew on the Cut. He went through it over to his block and then went behind the yellow apartment house. He went through the cellar and out into the backyard next to it and behind the haunted house. It was always empty. They took turns breaking in through the back door to show they had courage. He went in because he knew he *didn't* have any courage any more. He went down the back steps where the lock was always busted and he stayed in the cellar. He didn't have any light to see by. He could hardly breathe from running. He could hardly breathe because he was so scared of the bald guy killing him. He thought about cops checking on the car in the middle of Ocean Avenue. He was glad his pop was a cop in Manhattan. He was sure there were spiders all over his legs. He tried to remember if they had snakes in Brooklyn. He tried to remember about tarantulas and vipers and asps. His toes were curled up in his sneakers. His fists were under his arms to keep them safe. He tried to breathe very softly. He listened for things that would bite him and for the bald guy who was going to kick the shit out of him and then take him to the cops if he still was alive. He listened very hard. He heard himself crying. He was disgusted with himself. But he fell asleep. When he woke up he was still scared but he was more scared of his parents. He went outside to get killed or die in jail or be kicked all over the house by his father. It was light out. It was hot. Birds were flying around and singing. Kids were playing. The Eskimo Pie truck came around. That meant it was four o'clock. The Good Humor man came at seven. It was the time it was supposed to be and nothing was wrong.

He went home. His mother said, "You've been playing in *coal!*" He didn't say anything because he didn't know there was any coal in their neighborhood or what it meant if there was. He didn't care. Nobody had killed him. When he came downstairs from a shower and he had clean clothes on his mother was drinking coffee in the kitchen and reading a book. She looked at him. She said, "Don't do *that* again. Whatever it was. Understand? Don't tell me and don't talk about it and don't ever do it again. Take better care of your life. Understand? If you were a grown-up, I'd put some schnapps in your coffee and make believe you didn't look like an escaped convict. I'll let you have a soda, and I'll make believe I'm reading this book. Instead of thinking about how crazy you might have been, doing whatever you did that I refuse to hear a word about." She looked up all of a sudden. "Unless you really better tell me?" Petey shook his head. She smiled again. "Well, good luck," she said.

So he stopped reading about Teddy Roosevelt and the Museum of Natural History. He thought about them waiting for his father to come off duty before they had dinner and how they hadn't talked about the trouble Petey had been in. He stopped thinking about that too. He looked around the library. Miz Demeter was talking to a sheriff's deputy. Pop came into the library too. Petey closed his eyes. He prayed. When he looked up they were gone. He laughed out loud. He started writing down notes about the Spanish-American War.

After school they went to the market. They bought chicken breasts. Pop said he'd got a recipe from Miz Bean for frying up chicken breasts. He said, "She got it from her friend in New York." Petey knew from the way he had said that and from the look on his face that things were not completely wonderful anymore. Miz Bean was going for a mature and modulated relationship again. Petey hated when she did that. It made Pop act like a bear. He could understand why Miz Bean didn't want to go steady with Pop. He was cool. He was tough. He was smarter than people thought. And if you were in any kind of simple trouble he was the person you needed. But he could embarrass you until you died in your socks. He needed to take some of that belly off. Petey wished Pop would lift weights or something. Maybe he should jog. He thought of Pop jogging. He thought about those skinny legs and that belly. He wanted to laugh. He didn't. He helped Pop keep an eye out for chicken breasts. He spotted the black man. He touched Pop in the back and pointed with his chin when Pop looked around. Pop squeezed his arm and grabbed a package of chicken. He got behind the old man in the checkout line. He was wearing a raincoat over a shirt and tie. Petey figured he had a sports jacket under the raincoat. His shoes were polished. He wore black rubbers over them. His black leather gloves were patched at the tips of some of the fingers. His face looked like a teacher's face. He acted like Pop when he paid for his food. He didn't see the kid behind the cash register. He made mistakes with his money. He was thinking about something else. They followed him out. This time Pop got close in behind the old maroon car. They went through the four corners and out past King's Settlement. Petey watched how the road curved very sharply where they lost him last time. This time they were closer. Pop explained how the old guy could turn to the right and if you were a little ways behind him he would get lost behind bushes and pine trees and be out of sight. This time they would be up his exhaust pipe, Pop said. Petey looked at Pop's face. He didn't ask why they were chasing him.

The maroon car stopped so Pop hit the brakes. He stopped too. When he saw where the old guy was going he backed up. They got out and looked from behind a falling-down barn. The old guy was parking his car outside a house that looked like something from Mill Basin in Brooklyn. His mother used to call them the Average American Dream Houses. It was like a long box made out of bricks that had a chimney attached to it near the garage. There were bushes in front and a little Sears metal shed and a TV antenna. There were grass and split-log fences and some little trees. It was total Mill Basin in the middle of noplace. "Beautiful," Pop said. "We'll be back."

When they got into the car and were turning around Petey said, "How come?"

Pop said, "He's part of the puzzle. The business with the maps and Nigger Holler?"

"What puzzle?"

"The *puzzle*," Pop answered. Petey knew that was all the answer he could get. He turned the radio on and he shut up. A brown truck was coming past them on Sergeant Magby Road near the house with all the geodesic shapes and DON'T TREAD ON ME. "I won't," Pop said. Petey looked into the brown truck that was going so slowly. It was the guy with the horrible teeth who hadn't wanted to tell them anything about Nigger Holler. Petey wanted to ask Pop if the guy with the teeth was part of it too. But Pop was probably thinking about Miz Bean dating the guy from New York again. Petey could tell from his face. He didn't ask anything else.

They ate dinner without saying much. Pop told him that the Sheriff's deputy had brought in the Sheriff's Department's final report on the library. He said the State Police were bringing theirs in tomorrow. He was hoping the fingerprints would show them something. "Trouble is," Pop said, "not many kids have their prints on file. Just the real monsters and part-time hoods. And of course the children of the staff." He said it horribly. He said it like he was eating someone's finger and he didn't mind that it still was attached and that it crunched.

Petey looked up. Pop was staring at his chicken. "They take our fingerprints?" Petey said.

"Don't you remember?"

Petey shook his head.

"Well," Pop said. Petey waited for him to talk about it some more. He didn't. They scraped and cleared and washed and dried and put things away and Pop didn't say anything else about how the children of people who worked in the school had their finger-prints on file. He wanted to ask why. He wanted to say that it didn't make any sense and he didn't remem-ber giving anybody his fingerprints. He didn't. He listened to Pop talk a little bit about Miz Bean and then Petey went up to do his homework. He was doing a math worksheet and he had to read social studies. He had to do a chapter in his English book. He was thinking about somebody rolling a kid's finger back and forth on a pad of ink and then rolling it on a piece of shiny white paper. He had gone to visit his father's precinct and they had done that to him for fun. He couldn't understand why anybody would do that to a kid for anything besides fun.

He stayed in his room. He talked to Pop later on. After a while they went to bed. Petey sat in front of his sketch pad. He looked at the castle. He turned the page over and waited for the right words. He was going to write Pop a note. He looked at the white rough page and then he turned the pad back so the castle showed. He left it on his desk. He put on his flannel shirt and the Irish sweater his mom had bought him. He put on heavy socks. He took Pop's gloves because they were warmer than his. He carried a Swiss Army knife in his coat pocket. He put a hat and a scarf in the other pocket. He wanted to take the gun. He almost did. But he didn't think he could come back if he took the gun. If they found him he would be in very big trouble if he had a gun. And if they found him they would take the gun. Even if they let him come home the gun would be gone forever. He wanted to know that maybe he could get his hands on it some time. He left it there. He listened to Pop snoring upstairs. He hadn't started to drift. The house was quiet and warm. Pop's snoring was part of it. He didn't want to go. But he went.

He knew he hadn't gone more than a mile and a half. Maybe he'd gone two miles. It felt like twenty. It wasn't snowing because it was too cold. He could see stars everyplace over him. There weren't any clouds and all the heat had gone up. There was blue-black sky and all the stars. They sat on the high branches of bare trees. They were in the evergreens when the wind blew their branches. The stars looked like ornaments on Christmas trees in the evergreens. The stars looked like glass in the maple and birch and beechwood and whatever else you called them. He had about sixteen things he wanted to think about the stars. Some of the stars were supposed to make the shape of a scorpion. He looked. The stars were a ripoff. They looked like stars. In the Hayden Planetarium in New York they could shine their arrows and turn their projector on and connect the dots and you could think the stars made sense. *But when you were out in them,* Petey thought. When you were out in them and it was cold and you were shaking and you couldn't really feel your toes moving then the stars were a ripoff like a lot of other lies.

The snow in the road squeaked. Wind was polishing the road. It might be so slippery by morning, they'd cancel school. He didn't want to think about school. He also didn't want to think about the trail he had made or the wall he had to finish near the barn or Pop carrying firewood that Petey had stacked or the time his mom took him and three friends to the Hayden Planetarium and one of them had barfed. Sidman had barfed. He thought about the old black guy in the car. If he walked all night on Sergeant Magby and some of the smaller roads he could get to the King's Settlement Road. But so what? He thought about the man on the telephone who said that black people were a curse. He thought about the hunters and how mad Pop had been. He thought about his fingerprints.

One time they were playing stickball on the block in Brooklyn. One of the guys was pitching on a bounce. A little kid was official catcher. That kept him quiet so his big brother could play. It was one sewer for a double and two for a home run. Somebody would call out, "Car!" Then they'd move over and let the car through and go back to playing. The traffic wasn't that bad there. It was a pretty good game for seven o'clock at night in the summertime with nothing to do. Ginsberg was at bat and Petey and Dix were in the outfield. Somebody shouted, "Car!" The pitch went anyway. The little official catcher kid let it go through. The pink Spaulding bounced off the radiator grille of the car. The car stopped right there in the middle of the street. Four very big guys with tight black tee shirts and baggy green pants with big pockets and shiny combat boots got out. They were all black guys. One of them had an earring on.

Ginsberg said, "Holy shit."

The guy with the ring said, "You talkin me moth-fuck? *Hey?*"

Ginsberg ran into his house. The official catcher went down Petey's driveway. Whoever was batting let the stick fall down and raised his hands like he was giving up. Dix disappeared.

Pop was looking out the front window. Petey saw him. He walked over to the black guy and looked at him. He was very big. His arms had tremendous muscles and there were veins all over them. They looked like baby snakes. The guy was smiling. Petey felt himself know he was safe because Pop was there and it was Petey's block. Petey said, "*I'm* talkin."

The guy was really handsome. He looked like a movie star. He bent down. Petey knew what he would do and that's what he did. Petey couldn't breathe any-more. He felt like he was on the bottom of the pool and his body wouldn't rise. The guy pulled this bowie knife out of his boot. It looked a foot long. The guy smiled again like a movie star. Petey listened under-water for the sound of the front door and Pop coming out. He didn't hear it.

"What you be saying? How you sorry you banged a ball off of my car? Want me to cut you other ball free too?"

Somebody laughed. It wasn't Petey.

The guy with the earring and the knife said, "What you be *say*in, honkette junior?"

Petey looked at the knife. He said, "Sorry." He expected to hear the bubbles when he talked.

"Louder."

"Sorry!" Petey shouted.

The guy put the knife in his boot. He said, "You too *small* to cut at. Wouldn't be nothing left but for sandwiches, I get done with the trimmin. And I do *not* eat pork. You dig on that?"

"Yes. Yeah. *Sir!*"

The guy winked. They all got back in the car. Petey stood on the curb. Then he sat down. He couldn't stand up. Pop was there. He was looking at him. He said, "Learn when you should really be quiet, will you? That was so dumb. That was dumb as hell." Pop had his gun in his hand. Petey wanted to say that he had known he'd be safe. All of a sudden he didn't know it. He didn't know how long it had taken Pop to get the gun. He didn't know how long it took the guy to see Pop standing on the porch with it. He didn't know if Pop had ever been there on the porch for the guy to see. He wanted to throw up.

He heard his mom on the porch. Everybody else was out on their porch too. But Mom didn't care. She was shouting at Pop: "You let him—you nearly let him get sliced to *bits*."

"I was there. I had the piece out. He was safe. And I didn't want some deal, they'd keep coming around to win back face."

"Face!"

"He had to *learn*, I wanted him to learn."

"Why don't you teach him something safe like other fathers? Teach him how to weld! Teach him how to catch the ball right!"

Petey turned around. He wondered what was wrong with how he caught.

Pop said, "He needed to learn this. And could you hold the voice down a little?"

"Nobody needs to learn that! And no I *can't* hold the voice down a little. And do you need to stand out there in the street with a *gun* in your hand?"

"He had to learn when to shut up. Everybody needs to learn that now and then, don't you think so?"

Ginsberg was out on his porch now. Petey thought about asking him what was wrong with the way he caught the ball. He couldn't figure out why he had his trumpet with him that he played like shit. Ginsberg lifted it and started to blow. He was playing a movie song. It was the song from *Star Wars*. One of the fathers on the block began to clap and call out "Yay!" Everybody else did too. Pop just laughed and laughed. Mom went in and slammed the front door hard.

Petey stopped on the road. He heard a fiddle and a guitar. Then he figured out he was also hearing an accordion. A lady who sounded fat shouted, "Come unto *me!*" It carried over the wind. Then everybody shouted that and then they sang it. "Come-un-to-*meee*."

The wooden fence there had a mailbox on it and a name. In the moonlight and starlight off the whiteness of the snow and in the light from the house he could read it. STAYNES. Under that it had aluminum glue-on letters that said FAITH N BEHOLDEN TAB. The singing came up. "*Meee*." His chest hurt from the cold air. He figured he knew what old people felt like. "*Eeee*." It got quiet. Crazy Christians in this house with all the lights on right beside the road, he would tell Pop. Pop would like the crazy Christians part. He would tell Pop they had parked their pickups around the side of the house so they looked like puppies or piglets all sucking on the mother. *"Eeee,"* they went. But Pop would scream *Why?* with his face all red and his teeth showing. They would get Miz Bean in and State Police and sheriffs and all kinds of shrinks from the county board of services and everyplace else. They would all scream *Why? "Eeee."*

A strong light made him go blind. His head hurt. It was like somebody slapping him. But it was a flashlight. It was a couple of flashlights. He could tell from the way they wobbled. He closed his eyes. He crossed his arms in front of him. His clothes were too heavy and thick so he had to let his arms fall down. A man said, "It's the nigger's kid."

Another man said, "It's the nigger-*lover's* kid."

"Same thing whichever way," the first man said. Petey thought of the hill across the road from their house. He had gone up that hill. He had sat there with Pop's revolver at night. Below where he had sat this man had dragged a deer. Pop had thrown them off their property. He was the man with the mustache and Petey was frightened of him. Petey was frightened of everything now. The cornheads at school had talked about poaching deer. You use a super-strong spotlight on the side of your car or you use one of those high-powered battery pack flashlights. You shine the light in their eyes and they stand there like Petey. Then you put the deershot into them. One guy's father used a .30-caliber carbine and fired seven shots into a twelve-point buck before he was dead. Petey didn't know what a twelve-point buck was but he was standing in the light like one and he was waiting for the hunter to squeeze one off.

The nigger's kid, had he said?

"Tell your father," the littler one said in the darkness. Everything was bright but there still was darkness all over. Petey remembered the littler one. He remembered the metal arm. He smelled his cigarettes on the wind. He smelled the mucous in his own nose. Everything was freezing up. His eyes were watering from the lights because he had them open now. He didn't want to miss anything. Tears came from the brightness of the lights. They froze on his face and his face felt stiff. The singing had stopped. A man was talking high through his nose and very loud. Petey thought of Reverend Staynes.

Reverend Staynes was saying, "We are not prejudiced."

"*I'm* not," someone called back. Some people laughed.

"We accept the Jews among our members if they behave like Christians and if any ever join."

"At nineteen percent interest," the other man called back. Somebody said, "Oy vey," and more people laughed.

"*Reductio*," Reverend Staynes said. He said, "We accept the Negro in his place."

"Down South," a different man said.

"Africa," a woman said.

"*Ad absurdum*," Reverend Staynes said. "We accept the differences among men, speaking seriously now.

God made men different. He made them all. But He loved the Anglo-Saxon heritage the best. Else, why not make Jesus born a Negro?"

Petey thought the door to the house must be open. It must be very hot in the little house, he thought. Because he could hear what they were singing and saying. And he could smell them. He really thought he could smell them sitting in some tiny living room in shirts like the Reverend Staynes's and overalls like the man with the horrible teeth wore and everything smelling like old jockstraps and towels in a gym plus the smell of tobacco and wet wood and wood burning hot in a black iron stove.

"Tell your father," the big hunter said. "Say we let you go but we're warning you."

Petey nodded. His leg broke. It felt broken and he was falling before he knew the man had kicked him. "Answer back properly when you're spoke."

"Yes," Petey said.

The littler hunter said, "You crying, kid?"

Petey nodded. He remembered. "Yes!" He was shaking all over. Everything that was part of him was moving.

"Geez," the littler one said. "Geez, kid. Tough." He laughed very high up in his head.

"Tell him," the big hunter said.

Petey said, "Yes."

The Reverend Staynes said, "Directly connected to the loss of virginity, the *pollution* of small children in profit-making films. The smut on library shelves is a cause and not, *ipso*, effect. Do you hear me?"

"I *love* you," a woman said.

"If you love me, then listen to me. If you hear me,

then assist me with deeds. Books by Negroes mired in filth are the product of their desire to not only mingle their darker blood with the race of God's elect, but of their desire to avenge themselves on those who love America the red *white* and blue. Doesn't say brown in there. Or black. But you go ahead and read this sewage if you can. You *read* this so-called *Great Negro Short Stories*. Or *this* illiterate trash, are you prepared for the assault? *Yellow Back Radio Broke Down.* No surprise the author calls himself Ishmael, is it? Only surprise is, he admits it. It is the Ishmaelites we *fight!* There are words here, and this book, I repeat, is on the shelves of the public high-school library. *Was* there. Until a child in Christ removed and brought it home. Saying, 'Reverend Staynes: is it right?' That's the question Christ's own baby asked me. So I read it. I tried to read it. And I found words I hadn't heard in the War. And we are still *in* the War, aren't we? And when they remove brainwashing from the classroom curriculum, and when they lift the untried and un-proved and unscientific atheist humanist theory of evolution from the laboratory and the textbook, and pornography by black men from the library shelves, and indecency from the minds of the young, only then is the War going to be over. Listen to me. Listen to me. Listen. We have to begin with the books. We have to begin with Mister John Steinbeck and Mister Kurt Vonnegut Junior and Mister J.D. Salinger and Mister Ishmael Reed and Mister Great Negro Short Stories. Listen to me. We pay the taxes. So I say, Render up to Caesar what is Caesar's, and let them have that share. Listen, now: I say, *But.* I say, *but* render up to God what is God's. That one's ours. Listen when I say we ought to think of keeping some of *that* part back for Jesus and the white man's cause. *Quod erat demonstrandum*. And back into place it all goes."

The flashlights went out. They didn't kick him anymore. They left him in the snow. He shook while they crunched away. They didn't go far. He heard them stamping on the floor of the house. The Reverend Staynes kept talking about books in the high-school library and the Bible. That was God's book. He couldn't find but one copy of that, in all the earthly books in the school. Petey thought of the cards lying on the library floor. He thought about Pop. The man had said, *Tell him*. Petey couldn't think of getting himself to anyone else.

He was walking before he knew he'd gotten up. He was running before he knew which direction he'd been walking in. He ran in the middle of the road with his head down. He looked in the blue moonlight for reflections. He looked behind him for the lights. They weren't coming. He didn't *see* them coming. He stopped to find out if he could hear them. All he could hear was himself. He was breathing so hard there was a creaking kind of pump noise at the end of every breath. He wondered if he was going to have a heart attack. He had heard of hearts bursting. He thought about standing there until he froze to death from blood all over his chin and lips and tongue. Pretty soon he could hear wind in the tops of the trees. He looked up. The stars that sat in the trees looked like they were blowing back and forth in the wind. The stars above the trees and in the spaces around them looked steady. So the sky was moving and not moving in separate pieces. That made the ground feel like it shifted. He fell down. He waited for his heart to burst. When it didn't he stood up. He got out the flashlight he'd taken from his bureau. He turned it on. Nothing happened. He wasn't surprised. He was the guy whose flashlight made things darker. Who else? He listened to hear the men with flashlights that did work and guns. They would shoot him like a twelve-point buck. They could do it. They could get in front of him and turn the lights into his eyes and blind him. They could put seven shots into him. They could shoot him in the stomach and the chest and the leg that still felt broken. They could leave his face alone. When they cut off his head and mounted it on one of those pieces of dark-stained wood they would leave it in the dooryard as a warning to Pop.

He was running again. He would like to ask his father what the warning was really about, he thought. He would have to remember what the Reverend Staynes had said about the books in the high-school library. He wondered if Pop would believe that the Reverend Staynes had trashed the card catalogues. It could be. It *could* be. It wasn't. But it *could* be the truth. It might as well be him, Petey thought. He thought that as he ran. He said it to himself while his nose dripped down on his lips and his mouth fell open in the ice-cold air. It-might-as-well-be-*him*. Petey knew there was a song that went that way. It-might-as-well-be-*him*. Except he didn't want to sing. He wanted to vomit and fall and go to sleep. His side was terrible now from a stitch in the ribs. His leg felt broken. His head felt like the hunters were slapping it. It-might-as-well-be-*him*. He wondered if the Reverend Staynes had fingerprints on file. He hoped not.

He hoped that Pop would think it-might-as-well-be-*him*. If they cut his head off and mounted it with all twelve points, whatever they were. If they tossed it onto the lawn. He wondered. If they did that would he still be able to talk? Would he say to Pop whatever he should know about the Reverend Staynes and the hunters and black people and the books in the high-school library? He could be a cartoon on Saturday TV for kids. Petey the Talking Head. Twelve points. With two deducted for getting home late.

He stood in front of the house until he could breathe without the pump noise in his chest. He was steady above the waist after five or ten minutes. He was frozen but steady. Under the waist he was shaking. His knees wouldn't stop. His pants were wet where he had pissed down his leg. Not because he was a baby, he said to himself. He just hadn't had a chance to stand still. He'd been *busy*. "I just haven't had a spare moment," he told the tree in front of their house. He giggled.

When he went in he heard Pop snoring. He was downstairs on the daybed. He had drifted a while and settled here. This was some of his deepest sleep. Petey went into the bathroom and took his clothes off. He didn't want to look in the mirror so he didn't use the lights. He got some hot water and soap onto a washcloth and he sponged himself down. By the time he was dry he was almost asleep. He got his clothes into the hamper in the pantry. He took his coat and boots upstairs so he wouldn't use the closet off the living room and wake Pop up. He put on underwear and got into bed. The bed was so good to come back to. It was like a hug. If they were going to arrest him for some kind of fingerprints on file then let them do it. He would sleep in this bed first. He wondered why the hunter called him *the nigger's kid*. He wondered if he was. He wondered if that was part of the reason his mother took off. Would everybody care if he really was a Negro person's kid? He wouldn't know what to do if he was. *I really wouldn't,* his voice said inside his brain. When he heard it the voice sounded so young and in so much trouble and so confused and plain damn stupid that he started to cry for whoever in the world could sound that way.

※　　※　　※

They drove to school. Pop didn't ask him about why he couldn't hold his head up. Petey knew he was limping on the leg the hunter had kicked but Pop just watched and didn't talk. The freezing rain held the roads. Petey almost told Pop how surprised he was by rain clouds because the sky had been so clear last night. He didn't. He didn't say anything. They drove very slowly on the icy roads and they skidded anyway. In school he told DiStefano he had scarlet fever. He saw Lugene and he wanted to say to her that he had rheumatic fever and croup. He said "polio" very loudly when she passed but she didn't look his way. In gym he saw that his leg was yellow and black and green under the knee. He got dizzy when he looked. He told the cornheads in gym that he tripped going up the steps. Nobody cared about it.

He waited in Miz Bean's office. He waited during

math and he waited during history. He waited during study hall but that was all right because he had to take study hall in the library. When Miz Bean came in she looked at him very hard. She went to her dark green file cabinet and looked at a schedule card. He figured it was his. She sat down and wrote passes. "These'll get you back into your classes tomorrow," she said. She looked at her desk and at him and at her watch. On the telephone she talked very low about going someplace and then she took her purse from the bottom drawer of the desk. "Come on," she said.

Petey didn't ask her why and he didn't ask her what she knew or how she knew it. He wanted to go with her. They went to his locker for his coat. They drove in her BMW on the two-lane blacktop until they were a town away from school. The morning ice had turned into slush and junk on the roads but Miz Bean never skidded. The streets looked dirty. Everything looked old. There were cutout paper turkeys on the restaurant windows and inside on the walls over the booths. Miz Bean ordered coffee and pie and she ordered him a hamburger and soda and pie. She ate and she watched him until he ate. She lit up a cigarette. He watched her smoke it. "I'm going to stop very soon," Miz Bean said.

Petey nodded. There was jukebox music about trucks and cowboys. "You should," he said.

"I will."

Petey took a deep breath. He said, "So what's up, Miz Bean?" He felt as cold as he'd felt last night when he listened to the Reverend Staynes and ran from the hunters. But they had let him go. He knew that. They could come and get him whenever they wanted to.

"Tell me about the library, why don't you, Petey?"

He got as cold as he could get. He didn't know if his heart was working anymore. He knew that most of his life was over. Maybe all of it was. It was like jumping into deep ocean and you know there's nothing under you except the ocean bottom off Riis Park and the tide going out and you're going to die in all that deep green water. "I trashed it," he said.

"Petey, I *know* that. I've known it for a while. Suspected it."

"That it was me?"

She lit another cigarette. He watched the smoke come out. He liked to watch her lips when she smoked. She nodded. She talked in little clouds of smoke.

"But why *me?*" He thought about the Faith and Beholden Tabernacle. *Eeee*. He felt that she was treating him unfairly. For a second he believed he might be innocent. Why not? Then he remembered. "The fingerprints came back, right?"

"No," she said. "We said that so maybe whoever did it would get frightened enough to confess. We don't have the kids' fingerprints. We were pretty unsubtle. No. It was this: whoever did it really liked books and respected the library. None of the books was damaged, really. It was somebody in a rage, but somebody who was used to keeping under control. Somebody was in trouble and he wanted to tell someone about it. And library cards tell you how to find things. They're about information. Throwing them around like that said—it said it to me, anyway: *I need to find something*. Or: *I need to get found*. Generally. Something like that. *I* thought so, anyway. I still do. All I had to do was put the getting-found stuff together with someone I knew who was upset enough but fundamentally nice enough to do what you did the way that you did it."

"I was the only guy?"

"No. No, there were enough people to think about. But I knew you. And you should have seen your face, sweetheart, when you helped clean up the library. You looked so sick. You looked a little bit the way you look now."

"Did you tell my pop?"

"No. I wonder if I need to, really."

"But you're going to."

She put her cigarette out. The smoke smelled sour. "Do you want more food, Petey?"

He shook his head. He thought his head would fall off and bounce down the aisle and the waitress would trip over it. Then somebody else besides the hunters from the tabernacle could stick it on some plywood and mount it on a wall. "No, thank you," he said.

Miz Bean said, "I told you a secret of mine. Did you ever discuss it with anyone?"

"No," he said. His chest began to thaw. He knew what Miz Bean was going to say. He also knew he was crying. The tears wouldn't freeze in the restaurant.

"I'm going to keep this secret to myself also. The way you did. On a condition."

"Yes."

"You have to talk to me."

"Yes."

"You have to tell me things about how you feel. You have to talk about living in the city, and your mother, and you coming here with your father. And school. And what you think about sometimes at night or when you're alone. What I—what scares you, maybe. What keeps you from getting too scared. Understand?"

"Yes."

She kept talking. His head was on his arms on the sticky table. He moved it to say yes. She said to him, "And every study hall period, you have to find one secret thing to do in the library that's a tremendous help. Nobody can know why you're doing it. But you have to do one thing a day. You tell me about it every day in my office after you do it, understand?"

He made the yes with his face hidden on his arms. Yes.

"And if you want to tell your father, then you just sit down and talk to him. All right?"

Yes.

"But you *have* to talk to me."

Yes.

"And we'll keep it a secret between us."

Yes.

He felt her hand on top of his head. It felt so good. He thought he could stand up and get onto his knees next to the table and ask her to marry his father so he could feel this way again whenever he wanted to. He thought of his mother, though. His head felt heavy under her hand. It felt like iron falling through his arms to hit the table.

"You can make it," Miz Bean said. He smelled a cigarette.

His head lay on his arms.

"Petey?"

Yes.

And two days later Miz Bean was talking to him in the office. They were talking again about talking. She was saying, "It's hard sometimes. I know. Petey, *I* know. You hear me?"

He was trying really hard to say what he figured she wanted to hear. It was like money he owed her. It was fair. He was trying to pay up. He said, "Like about the baby. The baby you said—"

"That's right."

"I couldn't understand why you told me that."

"Think of it like money," Miz Bean said. Petey felt his mouth open. He shut it. "I wanted to give you something for free. Say I gave you five dollars right now. You'd figure, either I'm trying to buy something, or I want to trick you, or I just want you to have it. So I gave you that information. You took your time and you figured out there wasn't anything I was trying to trick you into. Right?"

He nodded.

"And you tried to figure out what I might be trying to buy that you wouldn't give me anyway, right? And you'd give me what I needed if you could do it, wouldn't you?"

He nodded. His throat hurt and his eyes hurt. He didn't want to cry. But when she said that he thought that he would.

"So by now maybe you're beginning to think: she just *gave* it to me. Go spend it, she said. She needed to give it and she gave it and then she said spend it, if you want. So I'll spend it. Except you won't. You won't tell anyone because you're my friend and you don't want me to be hurt or embarrassed. Right?"

He nodded.

"So that's why I told you. Five bucks for free plus a bonus. Because you find something out about me and then you get to find something out about you, and maybe something about *us*."

Petey cleared his throat. He said, "Thank you." He nodded his head and said, "Thank you. You know?"

Now it looked like Miz Bean was going to start. She looked down at her desk and then she looked up. She said, "You want a kiss?"

She came around her desk and she stood in front of him. She bent down and kissed him on the side of his head. Petey closed his eyes. She said, "We get caught like this, it'll *really* start talk."

Petey said, "I won't tell."

"Oh, I know you won't."

He said, "I don't have the right words for it, anyway."

Miz Bean went back to her desk, saying, "I have to remember to get my car down to Oneonta. There's a recall, wouldn't you know. The seats bend under stress."

"And you got enough of that," Petey said. He knew she wanted him to. So they began to laugh because they were so glad not to be talking anymore, he figured.

But she couldn't stop. She said, "Why don't you ask me about your father?"

"About how come you figured out it was me but he didn't?"

"You think he already *did* figure it out?" She smiled. "You think maybe he's not so dumb?"

Petey said, "I figured that when you knew, he knew. He told you, or you told him. Because of your being friends and everything. I figured you both knew but he wasn't sure. But he thought so. I've been scared shitless about him telling me. I've been going to bed at eight o'clock."

"Yes. So you wouldn't have to talk about it. He told me."

"Because he does know."

"Yes," she said.

"He *jumps* when he knows something like that usually."

She shook her head. "You're in so much trouble," she said. "So he is too. He has been, for as long as you. In suffering, these days, you boys are brothers. You might as well know that.

"Yeah," he said. "But one of these days, he's gonna get tired of brothering and decide to do a little *fathering*. Then he'll jump. All over my flattened-out body."

"Listen, pal," Miz Bean said. She stared at him. "You did earn it, didn't you?"

Pop wore his suit. The jacket didn't close without the vent opening up above his ass. He had decided to leave his jacket open. He wore a red tie with his gray suit and he looked like a detective. Petey remembered him going out like that when he had to be in court. His mom used to call it the testimony suit. Pop had the turkey in the oven and stuffing in the turkey and bourbon in a glass. There was a bottle of wine on the table. Petey set the table. He didn't wear a tie but Pop had made him put good pants on. It was snowing when Miz Bean came and she brought snow inside with her. She smelled like perfume and snow. Pop poured white wine for her and soda for Petey and he put music on the record player. His face was red and his head looked a little sweaty. Miz Bean looked tall with big shoulders. Her legs showed a lot when she sat down and

Pop looked at them. Her dress closed up to her neck. Her hair was on top of her head. Every time he looked at her legs Petey checked Pop. Pop was looking at them too.

"I wish I could've done some of the cooking with you," Miz Bean said.

"You can do the brussels sprouts with me," Pop said. "But I want you to be a guest today, not a cook."

"Brussels sprouts?" Petey said.

"And sweet potatoes," Pop said.

Petey said, "Yech," but then he said, "Excuse me." When he went upstairs Miz Bean winked at him. She didn't have to. He trusted her. He knew she wouldn't talk about it with Pop. Upstairs he watched the Giants play Detroit. He heard Pop and Miz Bean through the heating grate. The Giants were losing but their defense was making some plays. They were going to win, Petey decided. He was going to watch them win even if he had to come to dinner late. He was going to see the entire city of New York and its New Jersey suburbs win a football game in the middle of some cornhead place named Detroit. Miz Bean was laughing. So was Pop. They sounded good together. They usually did. They only didn't when Miz Bean went around with anybody else. Petey wondered why she had to do that. But she had to. Pop hated it. The kids Pop hassled when Miz Bean was taking off on him were in pretty much trouble without trying. So was Petey. But now Pop was rumbling and happy and clanking the ice in his glass. He heard Miz Bean say yes to a Manhattan when Pop offered to make one. He was glad to hear her switch from wine to a city drink.

Pop started talking about his master's degree. Petey

knew he wanted it even up here in the land of the cornheads. He wanted to be a history teacher instead of chasing guys with cigarettes or dope or knives. He was telling Miz Bean some more about Nigger Holler. Petey heard him go to the living room hutch to get the photo of the Nigger Holler church. "There's a black guy," Pop said, "he lives a ways from here. Sergeant Magby Road runs into some other road that comes out near his road. I'll show you on the map. I think this guy, he's about sixty-five, I guess, maybe older. I think he could be related to some of the people who used to live in the Holler. And if he is, I figure he's the great-great-grandson of slaves. See, *I* think the Holler was settled by runaway slaves off of the Underground Railroad. *I* figure there's a story in what he remembers. Maybe he's got family records or something. *I* figure some prof up at Syracuse wants an article out of it. Which he can have, with my name under his. After I finish using the guy's—story? Memories. Whatever he's got. For a master's degree, or a thesis if they want you to write a thesis. Otherwise, just research. It gives you an edge, they hear you have this *research* going on. I transfer what I can from N.Y.U. I take a night course next term at Oneonta. I start in with the education courses. I arrange to student-teach here, see? And then I start in going to Syracuse. I couldn't need that many courses. And pretty soon I'm an M.A., and I'm certified, and I'm teaching instead of beating up salami-for-brains in the hallways."

Brunner completed a pass for the Giants. Petey figured the poor guy had to be thrilled to not get any more intercepted. So, a four-yard pass. At least he remembered who his tight end was for a change. "Detective stuff," Miz Bean was saying. "I thought it was all your old *I'm a detective, I find things* number." When she imitated Pop's voice Miz Bean's voice got so low down in her throat that she sounded sexy. Petey waited for her to do it again.

But Pop talked more. He said, "It really did start that way. It was something to keep me busy that wasn't just banging heads and chasing truants, watching kids in all-day detention selling joints to each other in red plastic pencil boxes. I wanted—"

Miz Bean sounded the way she had sounded in the restaurant with Petey. "What, Sluggo?"

"Who?"

"Oh. When you put on that big jaw and go red, you look like you're worried about looking like a roughneck. You look like Sluggo. Remember the old *Nancy* comics?"

"Sluggo, huh?"

"Sluggo."

"Yeah. Well, okay. I wanted to feel like I was using my head. I'm living with this boy, he doesn't talk to me a lot because he thinks I stole him from his mother. All I am is a cop to him and the zoo parade in school. And you."

"Me?"

"Well."

"You're not doing all this Nigger Holler stuff for me."

"I'm doing it for me. But you might as well know about everything else that could pass for a reason. Who knows, Lizzie? I learned that in the cops. Who knows? People don't do things for cause-and-effect the way the social workers have been trying to tell us for fifty years. You know: a guy's poor, his life's tough, he rapes a baby. Or, he's deprived of reading matter so he sells smack. Jew in a PR neighborhood? He runs amok with a World War II machete. You know? I mean, all of that is so—made *up*. They make it up after the fact. It's an explanation. No, no: it's a story. I mean, like a novel. It's fiction. Guys get nuts for so many reasons, all you do, you arrest one, you get him off the street and into someplace soft where he won't break his head. He rapes the baby, some guys'd push him off the fucking pier and say he jumped. That's *true*. But you don't get reasons. Never, almost. I think it's too complicated, Lizzie."

"Maybe. Maybe with baby rapers. Do we have to talk like that? But you're not doing it because you don't think you're—well, yes. Yes, yes you are. You don't think you're quite good enough. Don't you hate it when we lay your life out for you like a long tongue someone's sticking out at you? But it's right. Right? You're doing it because of Petey and his mother and me and of *course* Miss LaBoobs in the history department, and half of the people you've met in your life. You're doing it because of whyever you were a policeman, aren't you? I thought you were much more sure of yourself when I first met you. The first few times. But you never told me this much before. Is that my Thanksgiving present?"

"If it is, it might have to carry over for Christmas too. I don't think I'm much more interesting."

Jennings kicked the ball about seventy yards to close the half out and Petey thought maybe the Giants would squeeze Jennings's head in because they were so happy. He felt them winning when they ran off the field. It was halftime but he was thinking about his

mom and what Pop had said. Petey hadn't been thinking that Pop stole him from his mother because when
Pop had explained what happened it hadn't come out
that way. It had come out that his mom had to leave
and you couldn't really explain all about these things
but she loved him just the same and they were going
up to the country where he could learn how to fish.
Ass-apples. He had fished off forty-foot boats going out
of Sheepshead Bay. He didn't need cornhead country
for fishing. He knew that. Now he nearly knew something else. He felt like Pop when he would say, *I'm a
detective, I look for things*. He said it to himself the
way Miz Bean had said it when she imitated Pop. He
felt pretty much on the edge of knowing something.
And he knew the Giants were going to win. That was
two things he almost knew. He also knew about the
library and the hunters outside Reverend Staynes's
Faith and Beholden Tabernacle. He couldn't talk
about the library. He couldn't tell Pop about the hunters who had called him the nigger's kid because he
couldn't tell Pop how he drifted outside while Pop
drifted inside. He couldn't talk about his mom either
because he didn't know what to think or if he wanted
to know. Something was going to happen and he was
going to find out things. Meanwhile the Giants were
going to beat Detroit. El Poop predicts the future.

It started to melt and get warm toward Christmas.
Petey and Miz Bean decided they would get Pop a
sports coat that closed. That was what they would talk
about sometimes after Petey sat in her office and they
kept each other company. He went to study hall in the
library and did whatever good he could. He found
books out of place and he put them back. He inter-

rupted a dope deal and pretended it was by accident.
The guys who were dealing were small but he still
worried about somebody breaking something off his
body after school or in the showers after gym. Pop left
him home about ten days before Christmas and went
down to find the black guy. He had application forms
from Oneonta and Syracuse and transcripts from
N.Y.U. He was going to do it. Miz Bean told Petey
that people should get hold of their dreams if they
could. Petey was getting tired of dreams. He was having a lot of them. He wasn't going up the hill with
Pop's gun. It surprised him a little bit that he didn't
want to. But he didn't think about it a lot. Once in a
while he would make sure the pistol was there. He
wasn't going outside at night at all. He was scared. He
waited for the hunters. Before he fell asleep he would
wait for the little one with the metal arm to open up
his bedroom window and put his hook inside and rip
it into Petey's ankle and start to pull. But he didn't say
anything to Pop except to ask about the phone calls
not coming anymore. Pop told him cranks went in
cycles. He said to wait for a full moon and maybe
they'd hear from their friend again. Petey waited for
Pop to smile so he could stop thinking about the telephone ringing late at night. Pop didn't. Petey didn't.
And when he fell asleep he would think about the
window opening and the hook snaking in. He would
think about the other hunter's arm crawling in finger
by finger like a long strong white spider.

When Pop came back the black man was in the car
with him. Petey was surprised. He tried to think how
he would feel if some big guy who used to be a cop
would come in and tell him he wanted to use the story

of him and his parents and their parents so he could change his job and feel better about his life. Petey was surprised again. For a second he couldn't wait to start telling the man about himself. Then he remembered who he was and who Pop was and who would be telling and who would be listening.

Petey stayed at the grate in his floor. He heard them rattling cups in the kitchen. He heard the other man laugh. It was the kind of laugh you laugh when you're being polite. Petey figured the man thought his father was crazy. But he had come there. He was in the kitchen there and laughing out loud. They had come into the living room and Petey lay on the floor with his homework next to him in case he was found. He wanted to look innocent. His head was near the grate and he listened.

Pop called the other man Mr. O'Nolan. He was very polite. He also sounded like a cop. Petey wondered if O'Nolan knew that. Petey expected to hear the pages of a notebook turn over when Pop and Mr. O'Nolan talked. "Good heavens, no," Mr. O'Nolan said. He laughed again. This was a different laugh. He was having a good time now. "No," he said, "I don't miss a black community. If I did, I would go to live in one. There are a great many people, for example, in Syracuse, not seventy-five miles from here, who are extremely self-conscious about their negritude. Excuse me: blackness, if you prefer. May I ask you—have you heard of me?"

"I saw you," Pop said. "I saw you in the shopping center."

"It was you, then," Mr. O'Nolan said. "Were you following me on the King's Settlement Road one day?"

"I have to admit it," Pop said. "I apologize if I scared you."

"I evaded you," Mr. O'Nolan said. "I thought you were—"

"There are a few of those guys around here," Pop said.

"You know what I mean."

"Some of them took a deer down, about halfway through my front door."

"It wasn't poaching or unsafe hunting practices I thought about," Mr. O'Nolan said.

Petey figured they looked away from each other and down at their coffee or tea. He was betting on tea. Pop liked it a lot. He was betting that they both looked down. He tried to see through the grate but the angle was wrong. All he could see was the daybed where Pop sometimes slept while Petey sometimes went outside with Pop's gun. Mr. O'Nolan said, "Have you heard of me from someone?"

Pop must have shaken his head.

"I was an educator," Mr. O'Nolan said. "I taught in the Metuchen, New Jersey, public school system for forty years."

Pop said, "New Jersey?"

Mr. O'Nolan began to laugh. He interrupted his own laughing to talk and then he interrupted his own talking to laugh. He said, "So, of course, I smiled beneficently and came along with you." He laughed. "Because I was only too glad to assist your researches." He laughed more. Petey heard somebody slurping at tea. "For if I am not the residue—could *dregs* be opportune though not wholly accurate?—if I am not what is left of a line of slaves escaped by way of the Underground Railroad, I am nevertheless indeed the descendant of slaves. Manumitted, unfortunately, quite early in the national history. Sent north and east, alas, with the family's eldest son, to take over a mill he had won, so goes the family Bible and word-of-mouth legacy, in a week-long card game. I have to tell you: I am born in New Jersey, bred in New Jersey, raised and educated in New Jersey, and then married there, employed there, widowed there, and lately come from there within the year to live more proximate to Raymond, my son, who is a chemist with the Norwich-Eaton pharmaceuticals firm nearby. You know of them? I am so sorry," Mr. O'Nolan said. He laughed so hard that Petey thought he would choke. Petey wondered if Pop would get up and put his teacup on the table and rip Mr. O'Nolan's ears off for not being from runaway slaves so he could tell Pop all about the history of Nigger Holler so Pop could write a thesis at Syracuse University and feel like the equal of a high-school teacher. Petey tried to understand why anybody wanted to feel like a high-school teacher. Mr. O'Nolan was stopping his laughter. Petey almost joined in on what was left.

Pop said, "Metuchen, New Jersey?"

"Near Rahway."

"Beautiful."

"Highly industrialized these days, alas."

"No," Pop said. "It's beautiful. I can close my eyes and see myself standing in front of your door. Did I ask you if I could take a sputum sample and a vial of blood?"

"Not quite," Mr. O'Nolan said. "Nearly."

"So, Mr. O'Nolan," Pop said. "Could I ask you this: how come you came?"

"I haven't—I don't mean to disparage the local ambience, mind you. There are people here who seem to be decent and hard-working folk. There *are* some backward ones. They're so white! I don't mean to speak racially," Mr. O'Nolan said.

"You mean they're undernourished," Pop said. "They live on potatoes and ice cream made of paper products mixed with soy bean. They live on food stamps and cigarettes. They're almost blue, aren't they, some of them?"

"Precisely," Mr. O'Nolan said. Petey nodded. He was thinking of some of the cornheads. Even Lugene didn't have too much color to her except for freckles. "And it was a pleasure to be spoken to as what I appear to be—a man of color—in a direct fashion. To be sure, I'd far more have appreciated being spoken to as if I were the same pink-beige as you. But your forthrightness, and your nervousness, and your vocabulary—"

"*My* vocabulary?"

"Indeed," Mr. O'Nolan said. "It pleased me to look forward to a conversation with a man of some learning."

"Me?"

"What do you teach at the high school?"

Petey waited for Pop to lie.

Pop said, "I don't teach."

Petey wanted to give Pop something he needed.

"You did tell me that you worked at the—"

"Discipline, I guess you'd say," Pop said. "Respect

for the rules. Fear? I used to be a cop, Mr. O'Nolan. In New York. I retired around the same time my wife and I split up. Petey and I came up here and I found work in the high school. I'm on the guidance staff. I'm the guy in charge of the monsters in detention and the dope smokers who show up for a year of in-school suspension. I break up fights. I chase the girls who carry knives in the halls. I'm the hit man, you could say. I need about twelve credits for my master's in history. I got my A.B. at night."

"At John Jay?" Mr. O'Nolan said.

"And N.Y.U. You heard of John Jay?"

"Fine school. I taught there once, at night, of course. I moonlighted. I offered a course in the American family. My students, some of them, I thought excellent."

"You must have a lot of credits, is that right?"

"I have the doctorate in education, Ed.D., from Fairleigh Dickinson University," Mr. O'Nolan said. "Were the times different, I might have been a professor, say, at Rutgers. As it was, I was pleased to teach social studies in Metuchen. And you are pursuing your graduate degree? I fully approve. May I help? To make up for not having hopped off the Underground Railroad and into your dissertation?" Mr. O'Nolan laughed again and so did Pop.

Pop said, "Have a drink with me, Mr. O'Nolan. That'd be a help. I'm embarrassed as hell."

"Alas," Mr. O'Nolan said, "Raymond, my son, and his wife, Agatha, expect me for dinner. I'm expected in—good heavens, an hour, very nearly. Perhaps you'll join *me*, for dinner, and with your son as well?"

"How about I call you, or I drop in?"

"Because you *do* know where I live, do you not?" Mr. O'Nolan laughed again.

"And we arrange something? This week? Maybe next?"

"I would be pleased," Mr. O'Nolan said.

They went out of the room. Petey stayed at the grate. The front door shut and then the car started. Petey went back to work. He was trying to figure out what he'd heard in Pop's voice. He couldn't. He finished his homework. He started to read social slops but he didn't want to. He wondered what Mr. O'Nolan would tell a class full of cops in a course named the American Family. How could there be that much to say? He turned the TV set on. The channel was getting "Sesame Street." One of the little kids was hugging Big Bird. Petey looked up at the window. Pop had a friend! It was like with Miz Bean and maybe it was better. Because sometimes Pop was afraid of messing it up with Miz Bean. Petey looked at the window while Big Bird sang and he thought about Pop thinking he had found a new friend. Petey had no idea why he started crying. He wanted to stop before Pop came back from driving Mr. O'Nolan home. He stopped.

Pop had set a london broil out so Petey cut the fat the way Pop did and set the meat on the pan for broiling when Pop got back. He knew it was going to be a while because he knew Pop would stay and have a drink with Mr. O'Nolan if he could. Pop had this new friend. Petey smiled while he stabbed two potatoes with a knife so they wouldn't explode while they baked. He wished Miz Bean was coming for dinner or Mr. O'Nolan had stayed. That way he could cook three potatoes. Three still felt better than two. He turned the oven on and put the potatoes in. The telephone rang.

He didn't know why he knew who it was. He did. It was like pushing a button and something going off. Mr. O'Nolan had come and gone so now something was going to happen. He didn't say hello when he took it off the hook. He listened. They knew he was listening. He couldn't tell whose voice it was. "Nigger," they said to him.

Petey cleared his throat. They were listening for him. He said, "I'm a white person." Then he said, "So what?" He hadn't meant to say that. He also said, "I *can't* tell him." He had forgotten the hunter kicking him and then he remembered. He said, "Hello?"

Pop was home. Pop was behind him. Petey smelled whiskey and peanuts. Pop was big in the doorway and big in the kitchen. Petey's hand felt like a piece of stone when Pop took the phone away and the hand fell down. Pop said, "Who's this, please?"

Petey had to sit down.

Pop said, "Would you tell me that again, please?" He said, "Curse, right. Warning. *Oh,* well, of course. Jesus. Niggers and kikes all over, I know. Sure. Listen, pal." Pop was red. He had the sneer on his face. He said, "Listen." He waved at Petey. His hand was supposed to be telling Petey that everything would be all right. Petey kept his eye on the hand. He said, "I am a retired peace officer. I am armed. If anyone trespasses on my property or intimidates my son or makes an *effort* to intimidate him or me, I am going to shoot whoever it is. No warnings. No questions. Squeeze off and goodnight. Understand? Hey, I want you to bear in mind that my guests are covered by this policy. You understand me? Bang-bang and goodnight. For any of you or your friends. That's number one. Number two is, no more phone calls. I'm bringing in the telephone company security people and I'm calling the state cops. To start with. We can talk FBI, you feel like stepping up the pace." Pop said, "Yeah. Right. I understand about the black man's curse, already. Yeah. What I want to know is, do you guys understand about *my* curse. You hear me? You hear? No warnings. I shoot on sight starting now. So you might almost already be dead, asshole." Pop slammed the phone back onto the wall. Petey was bending over. His stomach hurt.

"Asshole," Pop said. He said, "Did he scare you, Pete?"

"Yes, sir."

"I don't blame you. Did you ever hear of the KKK? The Ku Klux Klan? Did they talk about them in school?"

"I heard of them. A little bit."

"All they deserve's a little bit. You know about them."

Petey nodded. Yes.

"They used to be more important. I mean, they used to carry more weight around here. They have a lot of members still, in the South, the Southwest. Hell, they have them in California and they have them here. Of course, they get all mixed in nowadays with American Nazi Party types and the crazies who don't pay taxes and shoot at the IRS and the Creationists and the freaks who dance with snakes at midnight and babble in different voices. There's a KKK chapter, I heard, in Syracuse. I heard about it a long time ago when we busted some creeps in the city. They had about a dozen shotguns and shells and handguns in the trunk of this completely rusted-out piece of garbage they were driving. A beat cop saw this thing at the curb and he looked it over. They had a hole rusted in the car, near the taillight. The hole went all the way through the trunk and the cop looks in and he sees guns. We came as back-up and by the time we got there they had these turkeys lying on the street, they had all these guns and ammo out, and this completely stoned black guy flies by, he's about four feet in the air, and he says to the one with the shotgun who's covering all the jerks on the ground while the other one goes over them for weapons, he says, "Baby, I *can* dig it. How much for all of it, cash and carry. I let you keep the cats already down on the ground." Pop looked at Petey. Petey tried to smile. Pop said, softer, "Anyway. Those guys were part of a KKK chapter from outside Syracuse. We found out there were a lot of nuts around here. The intelligence people found out. And now we know. These are KKK guys, Petey. That's what they told me. They want me to be scared."

"I'll be scared, Pop, if you don't feel like doing it."

"You're okay."

"I am?"

"And they will not burn a cross on our lawn."

"Why? There's too much snow?"

"There's too much me. I'm here." Pop showed his front teeth. He wasn't smiling. Then he did smile. He said, "I'll call the phone company if they call again."

"Where are they watching us from?"

"They're not watching us, Petey."

"How come they know about Mr. O'Nolan?"

133

"They said they knew about him?"

"They said, 'If he ain't your slave, sonny, then he's the trouble you're in.' That's who they meant, right?"

Pop didn't do anything with his face. Then he made it smile. Petey watched him. He felt ashamed. He was with the toughest man he knew including the hunter who kicked him. So he shouldn't have been scared. He shouldn't have been thinking about his mom. He was doing both. He made his head move. Yes.

Pop said, "I'll put the meat on. Thank you for putting in the potatoes. They smell terrific. We'll make some salad. You want the Green Goddess dressing tonight?"

Yes.

"And don't worry. All right?"

Yes.

"Petey, I'm *here*. Listen—special favor: I won't cook the flank steak too *bloody*. Understand? You get it? Bloody? It's a terrorism joke, Petey. Come on."

Yes.

❧   ❧   ❧

In school Petey was remembering that Pop hadn't yelled when he'd nodded his head. He remembered doing that. He remembered that Pop always picked a fight with him when he wasn't respectful. Depending on how ticked off Pop was to begin with almost anybody doing anything could be disrespectful. He'd been scared while he nodded. Pop hadn't wanted him to be scared. He wanted him calm no matter what was scaring him. Because Pop was there and he was taking care of Petey and being scared was being disrespectful to Pop. He hadn't yelled, though. So the KKK telephone call must be heavy-duty business even to Pop. Pop had told him not to say anything in school. It was nearly Christmas. The KKK was calling up his house. Trucks went by late at night very slowly. They sat still or Petey would lie still in bed and the heavy motors would go by. They went very slowly. It was like somebody looking at you. Petey couldn't help it. He knew he'd feel better if his mother was there too. He could calm her down.

Miz Demeter helped him find books on the KKK. He took a breath and got the green plastic pitcher from her office. The cornheads watched him. DiStefano or Green or somebody would say something. Miz Demeter watched him. He went to the fountain and filled the pitcher and brought it back. He watered the plants while they looked. He went back to his table and caught his breath. He copied things out of some of the books so it would look like he was working on a research project.

1924—5 million members of Klan.
Pulaski, Tennessee—KKK started 1864 Judge Jones.
Protection of widows and orphans of Confederate soldiers.
White robes for purity plus scare Negroes—ghosts.
Maintain supremacy of the white race.
"The Klan was born out of bloodshed, out of a real need to protect the Southern white man from the carpetbaggers—the Jew carpetbaggers. You know, of course, that the carpetbaggers was Jews, and they

come down here and teamed up with the Niggers and tried to take away everything that the white man had."

Petey was copying out what a man said in Florida in 1963 after a church blew up and four black children died. He felt like Pop. He was taking down clues. *I'm a detective, I find things*. He copied more. The man at the Klan meeting said:

"When I go out to kill rattlesnakes, I don't make no difference between little rattlesnakes and big rattlesnakes, because I know it is the nature of all rattlesnakes to be my enemies and to poison me if they can. So I kill 'em all, and if there's four less niggers tonight, then we're all better off. And they ain't little. They're fourteen or fifteen years old—old enough to have venereal disease."

Burning crosses—Somerville, New Jersey. Peekskill, New York. Stone Mountain, Georgia. Worcester, Massachusetts. Hyde Park, New York. Starke, Florida. Indianola, Mississippi. Waco, Texas. Salisbury, North Carolina. Erie, Pennsylvania.

He got bored with writing Nigger and Jew and Mulatto. He looked at a book by Albion Tourgée that Miz Demeter had found for him. It was about schoolteachers who the Klan was chasing. It was boring. The KKK was boring. Except they whipped people and broke their backs and burned their houses and pulled people out of their cars and killed them. They called up people on the phone.

Lugene Winton was in Miz Bean's office. She was crying. She wouldn't talk to Petey. He went back out into the hall. Then Lugene came out. She looked at him. Her face looked bigger. She looked older. Pop had said girls their age grew up before boys their age. Lugene looked like someone growing up. He went in. Miz Bean was blowing her nose.

"You get upset a lot, for a guidance counselor," he said.

"Don't I?"

"Did you always?"

"Almost. I was once the school psychologist of an entire college. I was even a kind of dean. It was a very small college. It's upstate from here."

"So why'd you come here? From a college? Isn't a college higher to be in?"

"Only for the students. Sometimes. Why did I come here: I came here because I quit that college and went to a different one. In New England. I cried *all* the time, there, though. I was something of a mess."

"You don't cry all the time here."

"No," she said. "That's how I know I'm getting better."

Petey said, "I can usually stop crying when I have to."

"Oh, I know."

"I watered the plants in the library today."

"Not with your tears, I assume."

"You all right, Miz Bean?"

"I'm all right, Petey. Thanks for asking. Are you?"

"Oh, yeah. Sure. Pop tell you about the telephone calls?"

"Telephone calls?"

"Didn't he tell you?"

"Your mother?"

Petey's stomach jumped. He said, "It's the Ku Klux *Klan*, Miz Bean!"

She said, "Oh. Well, *that's* a relief." She started laughing. The way she did it frightened him. She had lipstick on her teeth. She shook her head. She shook it some more. "No," she said. She bit down on her lip and held her cheeks. "I'm sorry," she said, "I'm really not laughing at you at all. Will you forgive me? Please? Now. Now, tell me. The *Klan?*"

He didn't tell her about the hunters or anything else about at night alone or Reverend Staynes. He told about Mr. O'Nolan and the telephone calls.

Miz Bean said, "I think your father has a friend." She smiled. They smiled together.

Petey moved his hand toward her. "Two friends," he said. He hoped he didn't sound like he was begging a favor for Pop.

Miz Bean took hold of his hand and shook it. "Three," she said. They smiled and smiled. Then they talked about racism and psychological fears. He only understood about half of it and that half didn't have to do with why *he* felt as scared as he did. The bell rang. He was on the stairs and thinking about the stairs you went up to get to the BMT in Brooklyn. He was halfway to history before he thought about Miz Bean and who she had thought the phone calls were from. His stomach jumped.

They were talking about the Great Depression in class. He knew everything in the chapter. He loved it. He tried not to tell a lot of people. Some of them knew. His grades in history were the best he'd ever had. And it was fun. Miz Carver was pretty much not angry with him over Pop anymore so she called on him when his hand went up after she had talked about 1933.

He said, "This was, uh, Easter, there was this Easter thing in 1933. These—a thousand people in a field? Near Somerville, New Jersey? They burned this giant cross."

"Really!" Miz Carver said. "The KKK? In New Jersey. Well, they *were* active in the North."

"Yeah," Petey said. "Do you think that was part of the worsening social, uh—"

"Fabric?"

"Yeah. Fabric. Did they need scapegoats because of the Depression? Or is prejudice just part of American history? I was thinking—what the settlers, the colonists said about how evil the Indians were. It kind of sounded like the Klan, you know?"

In the back of the room a cornhead with a deep voice said, "No, man. Indians get drunk. Niggers gets *hah,* man." Everybody laughed. Petey laughed too. Miz Carver was screaming at them. Petey was under the noise. He remembered Miz Bean and how she laughed with relief. He was trying to figure out what she knew about his mother. He didn't know why it would be bad if his mother called up. He knew it wouldn't be bad for him. He smelled the perfume smell off her tight brown leather gloves when she was going out at night and kissing him goodbye. He thought of Mr. O'Nolan's hands. He thought they were the same color as the gloves. Except Mr. O'Nolan's hands would have fingerprints on them. Miz Carver screamed. Petey was hoping she wouldn't think he planned on this mess. He had enough problems already. He wondered if his mom had called before but nobody had told him. He didn't think he could ask. Pop might make him eat the telephone for dinner if he asked. He wondered if Miz Bean would tell him. He would have to act like a detective some more. He would have to look for things and find them.

They woke up on Thursday to a couple of feet of wet snow. The plow hadn't been up to their road. School was canceled. Everything was canceled except the birds. Pop stayed inside and paid bills. When he paid bills he acted the same way he acted when the hunters had been on their land. Petey put stale bread out for the birds and thought about the hunters. He decided that if they kicked you they wouldn't kill you. He said that to himself in Pop's voice. He got the shovel from the porch and started digging. He cleared the porch. He cleared the front walk to the road. He went along the road to the side yard. It didn't look like anyplace he had kicked a football barefoot while Pop had his drink and watched him. The snow was blown up in mounds and blown down in glinty patches. It was like a beach. Petey started to dig toward the barn so he could bring firewood back in the wheelbarrow. He figured Pop wouldn't think of that until the middle of the night.

It was exactly what he wanted to feel. He knew it after the first shovelful. It was like tight gloves fitting right. The shovel had a square bottom. It cut into the snow exactly. It came up perfectly filled. The snow was heavy so he dumped it carefully to the side instead of throwing it. He made it pile up in a wall along the channel he was cutting. He got down as close to the grass as he could. He made the channel wide enough for the wheelbarrow. The wind blew in his face and dried his sweat. He wasn't thinking about anything, he thought. The barn came a little bit closer. He felt strong.

While he dug Petey sang songs without moving his mouth. But his tongue and throat began to feel the singing. He didn't hear what he sang. He felt the rhythms and the words without listening to them. The channel kept moving. From time to time he stopped so he could look back and see what he had done. Sometimes he laid the back of the shovel on the mound of snow alongside the ditch so he could smooth it. Everything was very organized and the channel was wide enough to haul wood through and tall enough to be part of a battlefield. He began to think about sol-diers shooting from the trench. Then he thought about the hunters shooting back into the trench. He decided to stop that and he did. The wind moved in his face and the air was warm enough to smell. It smelled like the woods at night or the forest where his trail ended in the afternoon before Pop had his drink and they talked or made dinner. He was pretty sure his mother would love the field he was digging in and the woods where his trail went. He thought maybe in the barn where he had stacked their firewood she could have an old table and do things with flowerpots and plants there. He didn't think she ever would. The next time he looked up at the dark birch tree near their barn it had a dozen sparrows in it. They were puffed out against the wind and they looked like something that grew on the branches. Behind the tree all of a sudden he saw Miz Bean.

Her face was red and she was smiling and puffing. She was on cross-country skis. Her black slacks made her look taller. So did the way she moved her legs. She wore a short jacket with a white fur collar. Under the jacket her hips were moving with her legs and Petey watched them. When she got closer he switched to her face. Then he looked back to see her tracks trailing all the way along Sergeant Magby Road.

"I got lonely!" she shouted.

"Me too," Petey said.

"Really? Then isn't it lucky that I decided to come all the way up here and make you stop shoveling so you can talk to me? Well. I didn't come *all* the way up here on skis." She was still catching her breath. "I parked down at the bottom. The main roads are pretty well plowed. But I came up the whole five miles from the turnoff."

"Three," Petey said. "Almost three and a half, Miz Bean."

"You can call me Lizzie, don't you think? When we're off school?"

"It's a little easier if I don't call you much of anything too much," he said. "It can get confusing."

"Fair enough. Well, how's it going? How are *you* going?"

"I'm digging this trail so we can get wood out of the barn."

"That's a service," she said. "I don't want your father dropping dead from a snow-shoveler's heart attack when they've given us the whole day off."

"Is syphilis a venereal disease?"

"Oh, it absolutely is. You don't think—"

"I wouldn't know *how*," Petey said. He looked along her tracks. "I mean, I know the information how. But

I really—no. What I wanted to know is can a girl of fourteen or fifteen get venereal disease?"

Miz Bean nodded. "Yup. Absolutely. Anybody who has sexual contact with a diseased person can contract syphilis or gonorrhea. And genital herpes, I guess. I guess that's a venereal disease too. Who do you know who has it?"

Petey said, "I was reading about this church that blew up in Alabama. In the 1960s. Some black kids got killed." Miz Bean was agreeing with her face and head to show him she knew about the killings. "This Ku Klux Klan guy, he said it wasn't so bad because they were rattlesnakes and ought to be dead when they were young and anyway they were old enough to have venereal disease. They were fourteen, I think. Pretty gross, isn't it?"

Miz Bean said, "What a vicious statement. I didn't know about it. I never heard it. I knew about the murders. What, are you doing something on VD—no. On the KKK. For what's-her-name."

"Miz Carver? No. I was just reading about it."

"I hate to read about that stuff."

"Yeah. I stopped. I hated it too. Anyway, all the guys in the Klan—they're so *boring*. They all say the same thing. You know, there's a nigger, there's the nigger's kid."

"What?"

"You know," he said. "They think everybody's black whether they are or not."

"Do they?"

"Yes, ma'am."

"They're pretty frightened people, are they?"

"They are?"

She said, "I'd think so, Petey. Where's Officer Pops? Maybe we can get him to make me a cup of coffee."

She took her skis off and stuck them in the snow near Petey. He liked that because it meant she would have to come back near where he was working. She went in and Petey dug. After a while he was close to finished. His left arm and the small of his back felt tired. They came out of the house. Pop made a giant snowball and threw it at Petey and missed. Miz Bean had a bread tin and an empty cracker tin and she and Petey began making snow bricks for a fort. Miz Bean was very serious about it, he thought. She kept looking at him while they worked. She also looked at Pop. She would scoop up the heavy snow and make it even with the open end of the tin and then pass it along to Petey. He would figure out where to put it and then bang the closed end of the tin to make the snow come out. He would get the snow brick in position and toss the tin back to her. Meanwhile she was filling another one. They worked together. They didn't talk. Pop watched them. Once he went in for hot chocolate for everybody. Petey looked at the chocolate mustache around Pop's mouth. He remembered the time he and Pop had chocolate milk for dinner. Pop wouldn't drink his beer. It was a good quiet time. So was this one. Petey was turning the second corner with the bricks. Miz Bean said, "How did you know to let some of the bricks stick out for the corner like that?"

"I saw it someplace, I think," Petey said.

"*Homo faber,*" Miz Bean said.

"Homo?"

"Not homosexual," Miz Bean said. "Latin. *Homo—*

man. *Homo faber* means man the builder. That's you.
You make things."

She was sitting on her legs in the snow. It was like
having a girlfriend. It was also having a girl for a
friend. It was like having a big sister. It worried him
because it didn't only feel good. It was all of the other
things about women too. But Petey kept quiet and he
made the wall of the fort with their bricks. When the
fort was done on three sides Pop was on the other side
of the fort and Petey and Miz Bean were at the open
side. Pop made a face and started shouting. He came
charging at the fort and Petey closed his eyes because
he knew Pop was going to kick it in. When he opened
his eyes Pop was sailing over the wall like a big-belly
track-and-field star. He fell forward into the snow. His
coat was plastered with it. The wall was all right. Pop
wiped his mouth and said, "Once you get the touch,
you don't lose it. It's just like sex or riding a bicycle. I
forget which."

Miz Bean said something out of the corner of her
mouth. Petey wasn't sure what it was. He thought she
had said, "I didn't know you knew the difference."
Whatever it was Pop dumped a ton of snow on her and
she threw snow back. Petey watched. All of them were
on the same side of the fort.

Lugene Winton stopped going to school a week ear-
lier than Christmas vacation because she had mono-
nucleosis. She got paler and paler. Her eyes got red
around the edges. She stopped in the middle of the
staircase after the third mod and started to cry and
they took her out of school. DiStefano said she got
mono because of him. Petey said, "I didn't know a girl
could get mono because a guy jerked off too much."

145

DiStefano said, "Ain't you the guy who combs his palms?"

"At least I don't have to lick the fur on my arms, hair-pie," Petey said.

DiStefano stole Petey's clothes during gym. Petey found them in the locker room toilet. He had to wear gym shorts to his father's office. His father went home for clothes for him. He explained that he couldn't put DiStefano on in-school probation because it would look like playing favorites. Petey agreed. He bought pizza for lunch and smeared it on DiStefano's face right after they shook hands and laughed about how clever it was to steal someone's pants. When DiStefano lost his temper Petey kicked him in the leg the way the hunter had kicked him. On the way home he smiled and smiled. Pop didn't ask why.

He stopped smiling about the time Pop turned off Mason's Road. He was remembering a time when the little kid across the street in Brooklyn had bugged him. Petey was playing alone under the front porch and this shrimpy kid who whined all the time had found him. Petey told him to go away. He was playing war and he wanted to be alone in the game. The kid hung around and whined. Petey went into the house and came out with a fountain pen he had stuffed an ink cartridge into. He made the kid stand still. The kid was ready to do anything for a little attention. Petey wrote LEPER on the back of the kid's shirt three times. That night after there were some phone calls Petey's mother washed the shirt over and over with bleach. She never said anything to him but she made sure he stood there and watched. If his pop had asked him why he was smiling he would have told him

146

about the pizza. If he had asked why Petey had to stop smiling all of a sudden Petey didn't think he'd want to tell.

Mr. O'Nolan came over for dinner that night. They had a big steak and a bottle of wine Mr. O'Nolan brought. He was wearing the heavy sports coat and soft shirt and a tie. Pop was wearing a work shirt and khakis and his belly looked as big as it ever had. When he sucked it in he looked smooth in the front and tough. When he let the guts droop he looked even tougher but he looked like somebody who worked on the docks in Brooklyn and maybe had a quart of beer with dinner every night. Petey thought he was going to have to mention stomachs one of these days. Maybe he could get Miz Bean to say something.

Mr. O'Nolan was saying, "Wine is one of my favorite affectations. I know very little about it, and I don't even enjoy talking about it that much."

"You mean 'A bold and polished finish with a whatsit on the side'?" From Mr. O'Nolan's face Petey could tell that Pop had missed whatever he was aiming for.

"Exactly," Mr. O'Nolan said. Petey had known he would. He gave you every other minute like a present. "What I *do* like to do," Mr. O'Nolan said, "is to drink it. I have to confess that I am very much an aficionado. This Bordeaux, for example. It's a Pauillac, which is near the St. Emilion region. All those regions of the Médoc get mixed up. I have a hard time remembering them and I'm not even certain that you call a Médoc a Médoc if you can also call it a Pauillac. It gets pretentious. *I* get pretentious. But this Château Talbot, given to me by Raymond, my son, I've saved for a happy night such as this. It is a 1974, and Raymond couldn't

have known that 1974 was a fairly awful year. I read
that in a wine column by a man named Prial who is
most often a poet and never a bore about wines. Even
we can tell that the wine is nearly gone. Yes? You can
still get a magical small whiff now and again, the faint-
est taste. But it's gone. Liquid history, and it disap-
pears into the air. Still, it's worth drinking just for what
it remembers, even while it forgets. Am I right?"

"I have to tell you," Pop said. He had just stared at
Mr. O'Nolan. Then he had stared at the bottle. "I
know about good whiskies, and I don't drink junk. I
like some imported beers. You know the Communist
Chinese beer? It's a little gassy, but good and tough.
It reminds me of German beer. But I don't know anything about wine. I like red wine. Somebody pours
me out some white wine, I end up drinking that too.
I don't like it too sweet. Somebody pours me out some
sweet wine, I drink that."

"I do too," Mr. O'Nolan said. "But I'll tell you this,
I will one day open for us a bottle of Pommard I've
been saving. It's a Burgundy. I understand that very
little of it is bottled each year because it is a small
vineyard. I bought the bottle in New York in 1968 on
the advice of a friend at Fairleigh Dickinson. It's a
1964 Pommard and it's begging to be drunk. We'll
drink it. Peter, what will you drink?"

"I like wine," Petey said. "I like white wine. We
have this friend who drinks white wine."

Pop was blushing. Petey loved it. He listened to Pop
talk about Miz Bean. He wondered if Pop would talk
about Mom. He knew he wouldn't. He wished he
would, though. Mr. O'Nolan talked about his dead
wife and Petey felt sad for him. He watched the white

wrinkles on Mr. O'Nolan's knuckles move when he held up his glass or cut into the steak. He liked to watch them move. The skin was soft but it had these lines in them that were a tiny bit white. The only word he could think of was *precise*. Everything on Mr. O'Nolan's hands seemed to work exactly right. Everything on his body that you could see was soft and right. It was like oiled machinery. He never bumped into things or made noise. His glasses were clean and dark and Petey could see some of the houselights in them. He wondered if houselights made them get darker. His dark head was shining too. So were Pop's eyes.

They were talking about Nigger Holler and the KKK. Petey didn't want to hear anymore about the KKK. He was sure they'd get a call as soon as Mr. O'Nolan left. The last time they had called Pop had shouted out, "He's not a nigger! He's a mick like me! Goddamnit!"

Mr. O'Nolan said, "This is dreadfully harsh country. The climate is very cold and full of wind and moisture, as you well know. The summers are short. Spring is a flourish, an announcement, and then a departure into short summer. One walks, here, hunched over and one waits for the climate's blows to fall. One *lives* that way here, I think. As the climate makes us live inside our houses, we also live within ourselves a great deal. Do you see?"

Pop nodded. He was red and happy. Petey thought he looked like somebody who was hearing fairy tales. He looked like a kid who someone was telling stories to for the first time in a long time.

"So I am far from surprised to learn that racism here is strong. The people are as harsh as their land. The county is economically depressed. The farms have shrunk because of inflation, depression, and the growth of what they call agribusiness—you know the term? The enormous firms that run what used to be fifteen farms and thousands of acres, but now are run as one unit? Rural factories, I would call them. So people live in sheds here and in what they call mobile homes. Trailers, aren't they? Their livings are hard to get. They have no skills, so many of them. They have no trade. They have no education. Their lives are unsoftened by travel or new experience, except in some few cases by the military—but less and less, these days. Thus, they possess no analogy with which to adjust to phenomena outside their scrabble of lawn and family past. They know no reason. The music they listen to is commercial and essentially about disappointments like theirs. It reinforces their steady sense of loss. They feel sorry about themselves. They need someone to blame and someone to lord their rather lowly lives over. Needless to say, not a few of them assume that I made the move from Metuchen, New Jersey, to this hard country in order to provide them with such a figure. No. I cannot call myself surprised."

Petey said, "Are you scared?" He hadn't meant to. Pop's head turned fast to look. But he didn't look angry. He looked interested in Petey as well as Mr. O'Nolan. Petey felt proud. He wished he had some wine to sip while they had an adult conversation.

Mr. O'Nolan said, "Frequently." Petey waited. But that was all that Mr. O'Nolan said.

Pop went into the kitchen to make coffee. Mr. O'Nolan watched Petey clear the table. When Petey came back and sat down Mr. O'Nolan said, "I was watching you. I was remembering how my own son, Raymond, used to clear the table." Mr. O'Nolan smiled with his soft skin and white teeth. He said, "One evening, we broke the news to him that from now on he would have to assist in the evening clearing-up. He was eight, as I remember. Eight or nine. He would have to dry the dishes every night, he was told. Can you imagine what he did?"

Petey said, "He bellyached."

"He bitched like a private on KP," Mr. O'Nolan said. "But we stood firm. My wife and I."

"Responsibility's important for kids," Petey said.

"Exactly our sense of it." Mr. O'Nolan put his hand on top of Petey's. It was dry and warm. When he took his hand away Petey left his there in case Mr. O'Nolan wanted to do that again. "So we stood fast. That did not stop Raymond, may I add. He caviled and moaned. And do you know what his final statement of complaint was? Before he burst into terrible tears?"

Petey shook his head.

"My little black child, all wrists and neck, with hair as tight as the underside of a Kurdistan carpet, said, 'Didn't you hear, Daddy, that Abraham Lincoln freed all the slaves?'" Mr. O'Nolan laughed so hard that Pop came in. Mr. O'Nolan told him the story again. Pop laughed too. It felt to Petey like Pop was laughing at the story and also because it made Mr. O'Nolan so happy to tell it. That was the part that kept Petey smiling after he heard it again.

The telephone rang at eleven o'clock that night. Mr. O'Nolan had been gone for half an hour. Petey lay in bed and listened to his father walk to the phone. He didn't pick it up. Petey listened. It kept ringing. Pop picked it up after about twenty rings. Petey felt the air in the house stretch tight while they said things to Pop. He heard the telephone slam and ring when Pop hung up. But then he heard it dialing. The air stayed tight. Pop said, "Did you get home all right? No, nothing. I was worried about the wine, the ice on the road—you know. You're good? I'm terrific. A hell of a night. We'll talk. Okay. Thank you. Thank you. Yes. Thank you. Goodnight." He heard the phone hang up. He heard it lifted. He waited for Pop to dial the FBI and the telephone company. That was what you were supposed to do. But Pop hung the phone up again. Petey lay awake for a long time. He thought he heard trucks going by on the road. He knew that Pop would be drifting through the house. He knew that Pop was worried. He knew it was time for him to get really worried too. Except he already was. And he knew he was safer here than anyplace else. That was because of the footsteps his father trailed behind him in the house every time Petey woke up. Every time he woke he could hear them. He fell asleep listening to them. It felt like being in his fort but it also felt like being out on the Sergeant Magby Road with the hunters chasing him. He listened to the footsteps in his sleep.

HE HAD BOOKS on castles and drawings of castles
and a kid's game somebody in Brooklyn once gave him
where knights laid siege to a castle. He wasn't looking
at any of them anymore. He knew what to draw. He
was going slowly. He was getting every detail right.
The castle was built on a giant hill. There was a moat.
He would fill it in when he was done. Then there was
a wall called the outer curtain wall. They used stones
to build the side that faced in and the side that faced
out. When it was high they filled in between with
small stones and a kind of cement. They had a walk
behind the wall and they put merlons there. Those
were the high and low parts like the tops of rooks in
chess. The soldiers shot arrows from there and poured
down boiling water. Then there was the outer ward
behind the wall and then an inner curtain. That had
huge towers. Each one had three rooms and a spiral

staircase and narrow windows for shooting arrows down. There would be a dungeon in one tower and a chapel in another. There would be one with soldiers downstairs and a well and during a siege the lord and his family would be upstairs. The enemy would breach the outer curtain. The lord would vow to sell his life dearly. The men would be downstairs fighting for him. He would be with his wife and his son and his daughter. He would be wearing a tunic of chain mail. He would have a wound. His son would be wearing a sword and a dagger and a shield. The son and the father would stand in front of the wife with her white dress and the daughter would stand behind them too. The wife and the daughter would have daggers. The father and the son would stand between the women and the enemy. They would be waiting. He was putting every stone into his drawing and he was putting in every shadow. He was getting everything right.

Things speeded up and things slowed down. Petey heard his father tell Miz Bean not to open the mailbox across from the house without him. When Pop saw him listening he told Petey the same thing. Petey asked why. Pop said because. But Petey heard Pop telling Miz Bean about a guy in California who opened his mailbox and got bitten by a rattlesnake. Petey wondered for half a day why there would be snakes in the winter and how they could get into somebody's mailbox. Then he figured out Pop meant some kind of person would put them there. But he still didn't understand where anybody could get a snake from at that time of year. He went on his trail, and worked on his fort.

Mr. O'Nolan was teaching him how to play chess to

win. He was also teaching him how to play Monopoly and lose. "Any American boy can win or lose at chess," Mr. O'Nolan said. "But losing at Monopoly is an outrage to the North American soul. And winning is worse. It makes men monsters of pride and power. The only good winner at Monopoly whom I ever met is me." Mr. O'Nolan cleaned his eyeglasses with his wooly tie. "And *I* cheat and cuss and tip the board over if I have to admit I'm bankrupt," he said. "I have trained myself, however, not to crow over winning. For more than a day."

Pop and Mr. O'Nolan read maps together and looked in old histories of New York to learn about Nigger Holler. Pop called it the Hollow when he talked about it with Mr. O'Nolan. Then Mr. O'Nolan said, "Let us, friend, call a spade, as one might say, a spade. They actually term it Nigger Holler. Let's us too." They read about the McCann murder. A man in Nigger Holler killed another man for letting his chickens peck the killer's garden. He shot him with a rifle. Mr. O'Nolan said, "A curious history." Pop looked up. Miz Bean understood right away. She started grinning. Mr. O'Nolan said, "While I don't want to *doubt* the author of this book, he does write that the murder took place in December. What sort of garden might the fellow have to *lose* in December? What sort of masterful chickens could get their beaks into this ground in December?" Miz Bean nodded. Pop just stared. Mr. O'Nolan said, "Of course, I wasn't there, was I?"

That was the part of the time that went fast. It felt like living with a new uncle who all of a sudden was an old uncle you were used to. Except for the night with Raymond and Agatha everything went very fast.

At Raymond and Agatha's, after Mr. O'Nolan invited them to have dinner with his son and daughter-in-law, everything went very slow. The night took about three and a half weeks to get through.

Raymond lived in a wooden house near the pharmacy. Miz Bean talked about the gingerbread over the doorways. The carving looked like eyebrows to Petey. She pointed to the widow's walk and the little cabin on top of the flat roof. Petey liked the idea of the little cabin and of the widow walking out to hope her husband might still show up. He thought that only happened to sea captains' widows near the ocean, though. The nearest ocean was three hundred miles away at Riis Park in New York. But it was a pretty house with a huge Buick station wagon in the driveway and behind it a Subaru hatchback. Everything was painted and rich. Agatha was wearing something purple and silky that reached the floor. Her feet were bare. Her toenails were painted to match her dress. Raymond was very tall and very dark. You could see that he was angry when his eyes got narrow and he made a fake smile. He was as bald as his father. He looked like dark leather. He hated the whole night and he was having them there because of his father. Petey knew it. Agatha wasn't angry but she didn't care about them or anything. She was more beautiful than Miz Bean or his mother or any woman he knew.

They had to follow Mr. O'Nolan upstairs to look at his grandson who was asleep in his crib. He just looked like a fat little baby with nice arms. Then they had to look at Raymond's study. It was an extra bedroom with books and a big brass telescope on a stand near the window. Mr. O'Nolan was talking fast and loud and

Petey could tell and he knew Pop and Miz Bean could tell that Mr. O'Nolan was nervous and he wanted them to like his son and Agatha. He wanted Agatha and Raymond to like all of them. Petey could also tell it wasn't working out that way.

They went downstairs to the living room. It had three sofas in it. Everything was covered in white canvas. Raymond made drinks out of raspberry brandy and white wine. Pete watched Pop hold his breath after he swallowed some. Petey drank soda water with a piece of lemon floating in it. It looked like the bottom of the sink after a party. Raymond talked to Agatha and his father about the company. He kept calling it the company. Somebody was being fired and other people were being hired. "All ofays," Raymond said. He smiled at Agatha. She smiled back. She was so beautiful and she acted like they weren't there. Mr. O'Nolan looked upset.

Miz Bean had her legs crossed and Petey was looking at them. She said, "I haven't heard a black person call a white an ofay since I was in graduate school about a thousand years ago. Do you still really use that expression?"

Raymond looked at his father and then at Miz Bean. He said, "What expression?"

Agatha offered everybody a dish with chunks of salami that had toothpicks in them. Petey took one. He wanted about thirty. She kept the dish there and nodded with her dark eyebrows up. He took a few more. When she brought pickled hearts of artichokes around he said no thank you.

Pop said, "So what's your job like, Raymond?"

Raymond smiled when he answered. He didn't

mean it. "It's mostly ducking under low-flying office politics. Otherwise, I spend some time working up protocols with physicians who consult with us on product safety. I write in the kind of language designed to be seen only in agate type. What's your job like?"

Pop's chin went up in the air. He said, "I make sure bad boys and girls don't bother the teachers in the high school."

Miz Bean made a noise with her lips.

Mr. O'Nolan said, "Oh, now."

Agatha said, "I suppose it beats pumping gas for a living. Or cleaning chimneys out. Or shining shoes?"

Mr. O'Nolan said, "I wish I could *find* a good shoe shine in town."

Raymond said, "There are shines to be found, Daddy."

Miz Bean said, "That's another one I haven't heard since graduate school days. Do you use *that* expression a good deal?"

Raymond asked, "What expression?"

Then they went into the dining room. They ate without talking very much. Petey thought that the dinner would just keep going. Especially after they were done when Mr. O'Nolan said, "Agatha and Raymond. My gramercies for a fine meal. You're the kind hosts of my friends. I've wanted my *friends* to meet you."

Agatha said, "Oh, it's really nothing, believe me."

"Believe her," Raymond said.

Mr. O'Nolan opened his mouth but Pop interrupted him by saying, "*I* had a hell of a time. So thank you. But my boy's due for sleep, you understand?" Petey closed his eyes and waited to feel like anything else.

But he had to open them and smile. They had to leave. Pretty soon they did. Agatha put her cheek next to Miz Bean's but without touching it and she kissed the air behind Miz Bean's head while she said, *"Mmm."* Raymond held Pop's right hand in both of his hands. They were bigger than Pop's and it was like seeing a piece of bone sink into oil. Mr. O'Nolan stood at attention and nodded to Raymond and patted Agatha's cheek. He shook his head at Raymond. Raymond pretended not to see.

In the car Mr. O'Nolan said, "People do tend to work in categories. I've experienced a good many of them. I try not to hold it against them."

Miz Bean was in the back seat with Mr. O'Nolan. Petey turned around to find out from Mr. O'Nolan's face just what he had meant. He saw Miz Bean put her arm through Mr. O'Nolan's. She leaned over against him and kissed him on the cheek. He didn't smile but he did pat her hand. Pop said, "There's enough *real* enemies to worry about, huh?"

Mr. O'Nolan said, "Enough to rejoice in for real friends."

"Enough doubletalk to sink a ship on Oneida Lake," Miz Bean said. "Raymond went headhunting, and *we* was the heads." The grown-ups laughed and Mr. O'Nolan leaned over and kissed Miz Bean on the cheek.

"My son the shirt," Mr. O'Nolan said.

Pop said, "Shirt?"

"As in stuffed," Mr. O'Nolan said.

"And mounted," Miz Bean said.

Petey thought about a head that was stuffed and then mounted on a wall someplace.

So everything went fast except for that and except

for the scary stuff and that went much too slowly. You could feel everything that was happening in it. Professor Mulvaney didn't come to visit Miz Bean anymore. Pop and Miz Bean were together at the house with each other and Mr. O'Nolan a lot. There was another telephone call. Petey never answered the phone anymore. Pop took the call and listened. Petey and Mr. O'Nolan were in the kitchen. They watched Pop listen. Pop's face was white above the lips. His eyes were closed. He hung up the phone gently. He poured more whiskey into his glass and Mr. O'Nolan's. He said to Petey, "Wait here, please." Petey didn't move. They went into the living room. He heard Pop's voice. It was flat. It was like a soft heavy tire on top of gravel. It was like Pop was very sick. Petey heard some of the words about the Klan and calls and warnings. Mr. O'Nolan's voice was higher than Pop's. It bounced more. It carried longer words. They were about intimidation and provincialisms and the usual bigotries and Federal Bureau of Investigation.

That was when Pop said it. Petey heard it again. He moved closer to the doorway of the kitchen. He sat down on the chair under their wall phone. He leaned his head back against the wall near the telephone and he listened very carefully to Pop. He knew it was coming now.

Pop said, "It was a bitch of a separation. Understand? All the usual bad things about splitting up—money, car, fees for this and support for that. Apparently, it doesn't matter if your wife decides to fuck *two* other people on a fairly regular rotating basis. If you'll pardon the expression. What matters is, she tells the judge, her lady lawyer tells the judge, she is doing this

because the marriage is irreparably broken by the husband's infantile and excessively romantic attachment
to a dangerous occupation that has stunted his love of
hearth and home. I swear, this cigar-smoking bitch in
a black pantsuit with a *vest*, she has to shave I figure
three times a week just to appear on the street walking
her *dog*, the lawyer says 'hearth and home.' Also, she
no longer takes pleasure in marital relations, the lawyer says. And it's my fault! Never mind. Never mind.
It's all words. People have to find words to shove their
problems into. Everybody's sending messages in
bottles. Fine. What it means is we're done. She
knows, I know, the lawyer knows, the judge knows,
the lawyer's dog knows. Finished. The usual friendly
stuff after fourteen years of bliss. *Damn!* All of it wasn't
that bad, you know? But what I'm saying is, the judge
made it very clear to the lawyer, and the lawyer made
it very clear to my wife, and my wife made it very
clear to me, that they were going to give her my car,
my house, my neckties, my hair tonic, and inciden-
tally my son. Him! My baby out there! Because she
was having such a tough time with mental strain and
all, and she was so incapacitated for marital relations,
she happened to be fucking *two guys*. And one of them
was another *cop!* I'm sorry. *Damn*.

"I'm saying I stole him."

"You stole your son?"

"I took him up here with me while my wife was off
for two weeks with the guy she was fucking who wasn't
a cop. It was the separation. At the end of it, she was
coming home and taking Pete."

Mr. O'Nolan said, "You act quickly. My compli-
ments."

"Thanks."

"Intemperately, perhaps. But with real dispatch."

"No, please. No lectures about that, all right?"

"My friend, I wouldn't. I'm sorry if I seemed to. I use my words for props and costumes and camouflage as well as signals of sorts. You understand? I was embarrassed by the intimacy of your revelation."

"Yeah," Pop said. "Yeah, I was too, and I apologize for dumping that and asking you to carry it all around with you. You're my friend and I told you. Is that all right?"

"I'm honored," Mr. O'Nolan said. "Embarrassed. And richly honored."

"Baloney," Pop said. "Nothing I say to you is an honor for anybody except me." Then he said, "Do you think we should stop being so touching?"

"It would be a relief."

"You *can* be a hardass."

"Indeed."

Pop said, "I spent one more night crying. Then I got drunk. Then I threw up. In between I talked myself out of killing her. I also talked myself out of killing the guys. I figured Petey needed me more than I needed to kill them. I thought about it, though. I did. I got a good night's sleep. That left me with eleven days before she came home. I told myself, if I found somebody to buy the house and give me the money and still have enough time to get out of town, I was going. She could come home and find somebody else in the house and her clothing in storage along with whatever I decided not to take along. You know, second-best ashtrays, the broken blender, the black-and-white TV. I'd take Petey and we'd move, and they could hunt me down if they wanted me enough. You know the scary part? It wasn't too hard. Of course, cops are part crooks. All the best sociologists say that. The ones who go on TV. But it wasn't that hard. I told some realtors who never heard of me or my wife that I had to sell in a week because of an emergency. They said forget it. I upped the commission to ten percent and they got very earnest. I circulated the word at the precinct house. I told the guys at the union. I retired on the spot to get my pension in the works. I opened the safe-deposit box and took out the emergency money. I cashed in some certificates early. I asked for a few favors and I got them because I used to give out a few favors. I got into the evidence room for Rockland County because I had a cop friend who my wife wasn't fucking who lived on Long Island, he had some cop friends. I took two confiscated credit cards, stolen, forged, I don't know, I didn't care which. I figured we could live off them a while if we had to. And some guy from Cleveland who's getting transferred to New York and his wife is from Brooklyn, he takes the house! They're in Manhattan in a hotel, the realtor gets them down in three days, and zap: it's a deal. He maybe thought it was almost Park Slope, she knew it was Flatbush, they closed a day after my wife was supposed to come back, she came home two days late, you believe it? And they got a nice house. Too many blacks and PRs moving in, but okay."

"They decrease the value of real estate, I understand."

"Look how many times I lose my shirt in Monopoly when I play with you. Of *course* they tear down your real estate values. I had the stuff in storage, anyway, and all we had to do was move. She came home to a stripped house, we were in a hotel in White Plains, and by the time she figured out what was going on, we were upstate, she was running in circles, and the buyer's moving in. So we got here."

"And found this house. And had the money to buy it because you forced the *sub rosa* sale of your old house against all the odds I can imagine. You took your son, you found work, you made a home, you found Lizzie Bean, on whom I cannot refrain from congratulating you, and here you are. I follow your logic. I can see where you go. You could not possibly call the FBI and claim the violation of civil rights by a gang of thugs and bullies."

"That's what I was trying to tell you. Yes."

"They would investigate you as certainly as they would study the pathetic little pack of KKK on the Sergeant Magby Road. It must be pro forma."

"But it endangers *you*," Pop said. "I don't want something frightening or injurious—do you know what I'm worrying about?"

"Your worries are two. One is that something will happen to any of us, but especially to me because I am the nigger in the woodpile. The second is that you are worried lest it happen because of your circumstances. You endanger me. You are my friend, and you place me in straits. Of course, those very pale and mad other people are doing more than their own share. But you're frightened lest a friend cause pain, and conceivably worse, to a friend. And you are—I think the word might be mournful. Because it is a white friend who, willy nilly, enables other whites to threaten me, a black."

"I call for help, she'll sure as hell find out. She's got detectives after me. I'm sure of it. I figure she'll find me in a couple of weeks. If—you know."

"So, then. We'll have to manage on our own. Have you ideas?"

"I'm looking for them. I'm trying to hurry."

"I will too. We'll pool our resources. And do you think we might enlist Lizzie? She's a good deal brighter than either of us."

"I don't want her hurt too."

"Then tell her to stop seeing you. If they know when I'm here, they know when she's here."

"I know. I know."

"Lizzie too, then? The three of us?"

"And Petey," Pop said. "He's part of it. And he knows things about this road. About the area. He's got a trail down there you wouldn't believe. It's cleared off like a rug, at least it was last summer. He sneaked out once, I think, late at night. I think he might have seen something. He came back just about when I was ready to go after him. Or maybe I dreamed him going out. Maybe *he* dreamed him going out and we met in the dreams. I don't know. I remember, I was scared to hell. I think maybe he saw something and we should ask him."

"You're not proposing some kind of vendetta, with me slobbering through the snowy woods to leap on fascists and strangle them? You're not proposing a film?"

"These guys are real life. We're all of us too feeble and scared and smart to be part of something like that. Believe me, no. No. I'm talking—I don't know. We have to do something and maybe we can think of it."

Mr. O'Nolan said, "And will you tell Petey about how you stole him away?"

Pop was quiet. Then he said, "I'm afraid to. What if he decides to go back?"

That was one of the parts that nearly took forever.

Mr. O'Nolan said, "Don't tell Raymond, I think." Pop laughed. "He already knows you to be a honky redneck toad. If he thought you were leading his old man astray—"

Petey kept on hearing Pop say *What if he decides to go back?*

That was two days before Christmas. Mr. O'Nolan went to Raymond and Agatha's house for Christmas Eve. Miz Bean came to stay with them. It was another time that took a long time. Christmas Eve went on for sixteen years. Pop had told Miz Bean about the Klan. So if a snowmobile went by with a cornhead on top of it she jumped. They would ride on top like they were riding a horse over a hurdle. They wore black plastic helmets that covered their faces with black visors. They looked like spooks. They didn't come too close to the house but you could hear them. When trucks went by on their road Miz Bean stood still. When they went by slowly she stood there a longer time. When snowplows went by it was bad. They only sent them up once a day. They sent the oldest ones because the road was so tough on machinery. You could hear them coming two minutes before they got near the house. It was like something inside of the ground. When they were out front it was like the road blowing up. Miz Bean was drinking a lot of white wine and she was laughing a lot.

The Christmas tree was from their land. Petey had

picked it out. Pop had stood there with him and looked at it. Then they both got on their knees in the snow and pushed and pulled at the bush saw until the tree came down. It took Pop an hour to get it to stand straight in the metal gadget. He broke a pane of a living room window knocking it sideways when he got mad at it. They taped a cardboard from the back of a pad over the hole. Petey didn't say anything about breaking the glass. Miz Bean did. Petey left the room when she started.

After dinner on Christmas Eve Pop sat on the living room sofa and finished the wine. Miz Bean and Petey decorated the tree. Petey kept thinking about the two big cardboard boxes of ornaments and old toys that his mother used to make him drag down from the attic. She had told him she'd started saving ornaments the year after she and Pop got married. She used to tell him, "Your whole life's in there. Anyway, a lot of your life's in there. Some of the nicest parts." They had left the boxes in storage. Petey hadn't remembered about them and Pop probably hadn't cared. They were back in Brooklyn. Miz Bean had brought two big bags from the Ames. The cornheads all shopped there and at Jamesway for Christmas. They bought cheap perfume and games for their computer toys in their mobile homes that they couldn't afford. They bought Dacron-and-plastic shirts for each other. They bought cardboard shoes. They bought bright red ornaments that broke if you looked at them hard. They bought tinsel that cut your fingers. They bought Japanese robin redbreasts you could perch on a branch of your Christmas tree. They bought records of people singing songs about Christmas that were meant to make you cry.

Pop was smiling. But he kept his face moving toward the windows when trucks went by. But he was smiling. Miz Bean was nervous. She looped the electrical cords with little white bulbs on them around the middle of the tree. It was a fat tree and she had to try twice to get the cords right. Meanwhile his mom was in the city someplace and she was looking for him. All he had to do was get killed by the KKK and the FBI and the New York State Police and the Sheriff's Department would all come up with their sirens going. The word would get back to the city where she was sad about him. All he had to do was get wounded. If she came back it was possible that she and Pop would try and get together. Except his mom was fucking two men. He excused himself and went into the bathroom and brushed his teeth. He kept on spitting when he was done. He used Pop's mouthwash that tasted like Clorox. He still had to spit. If she came back something unhappy would happen to Miz Bean. She already had lost a baby. She could talk to his mother about that. Maybe they'd be friends. But it wouldn't be fair if Miz Bean had to lose Petey now, Petey thought. But it wouldn't be right that his mom had to lose him. But it wouldn't be right either if Pop had to lose him. *What if he decides to go back?*

Miz Bean was laughing a new kind of laugh. It was the way Lugene would laugh when she was hanging around with the juniors and seniors and they were talking about things that Petey figured had her scared. She wanted to look cool so she laughed. Miz Bean was drinking more wine and laughing that way. Pop was rumbling like the snow plow half a mile away. Petey went into the kitchen. Pop or Miz Bean had put a record on. It was Perry Como singing about Christmas. He always sounded like he meant it. Petey figured Perry Como would be all right as a father. He sounded like the kind who didn't shout. Petey tipped a jug of white wine and took a taste. It was sour but not bad. He took another taste. He went into the pantry and got the gun. He pulled his shirt out over his pants and tucked the gun into the waist of his jeans. He made sure the safety was on. He sneaked around the corner to the stairs. In his room he got the bullet. He loaded the gun.

He knew he wouldn't be able to sneak so he did it in the open. He moved fast once he got downstairs. He didn't wait to get boots on because that would slow him down. He grabbed his coat and called, "Excuse me, I'll be right back in, right back." He was out with the door closed behind him before they talked. He kept moving. It was black. He didn't see any stars or any moon. It was black and wet. It was going to snow and be a white Christmas. The plow was getting closer. His feet were wet from deep snow. They were cold. He put his coat on and zipped it while he walked. He went over the fence into snow that was higher than his knees in some places. He was really cold now. He went up the hill. The plow was making things shake. He could feel it coming. He didn't stop to catch his breath. He heard the door open and he felt the light come out onto the snow. He thought Pop was looking for him. He heard Miz Bean say, "Maybe let's let him be alone for a little while. This has to be such a difficult night."

He was up. The door was closed. He saw them through the living room windows. Pop was hugging Miz Bean. He was holding on to her. Petey remembered that his pop needed to hold on too. It probably wasn't Pop's most thrilling night either, Petey thought. Then he thought: *So. So. Tough shit.* Nobody asked him to run away. Except if he hadn't then Petey would be with his mom tonight. Except then he'd be worrying about where Pop was in some city someplace with snow falling on him and worrying about where Petey was.

He was at the top of the hill now. He was shivering. The ground was shivering from the plow. He could see the lights coming to the turn in the road before their property. He heard it roaring like an explosion. The sky was black. It wasn't fair.

The plow was there now. It was giant. It had lights all over it. It had four bright round headlights and a spotlight on the passenger side of the cab. It kept roaring and clanking. Everything shook. The snow exploded up in front of it and around it. Sparks shot up when the plow hit rocks. Petey didn't put the gun in his mouth. His mouth tasted very bad. He opened his mouth and let his breath steam out onto the barrel. He did that and then he put the barrel up onto his forehead. He reached around and pushed the chambers. He didn't spin hard. He pushed a little. He didn't have much strength in his hands. He pushed again and he slid the safety off. He kept the gun on his head. He kept his mouth open. The sound of the plow was all around the house and on the hill and all over him. His mouth was open and he was shouting at the plow. He was shouting with the plow. He was singing with the plow. He kept his eyes open. He was singing his Christmas Eve song with the plow and it was going past. The ground shook. He yanked on the trigger and the barrel jumped on his head. It didn't go off. It wasn't fair.

He was covered with sweat and noise and then the wind took them both from his face. It wasn't fair. He was shaking but the ground wasn't shaking anymore. The plow was past and everything was quiet except the whistle. It wasn't a whistle. *Eeee*. It was more like a high scream. It was. It was him. He made it stop. He took his hand down and put the safety on and put the gun into his coat pocket. He stood there and looked at the house. He waited to think something about his father and Miz Bean and his mother. He took the gun back out and slid the safety and pointed the gun at his knee. All he needed was a wound. He moved the gun so it was pointing at his foot. He shut his eyes and said, *"Agh!"* But he couldn't shoot. "Bang," he said. He put the gun away. He went back down. He knew that Pop probably wouldn't ask anything about where he'd been. Probably they had been sitting there and trying out the Christmas tree lights and deciding he was a troubled child. They'd probably leave him alone.

He went into the kitchen without looking around. He took the cartridge out and very quietly put the gun away in its cloth in the roasting pan. Nobody came in to ask him anything. He went upstairs and changed into dry socks and his old sneakers and a heavy sweater that Pop used to wear. When he came downstairs they were turning the Perry Como record over. Pop didn't look at him. Over his shoulder Pop said, "Wind kicking up?"

"Snow for Christmas," Petey told him.

Miz Bean stayed over. After Petey went to bed she went upstairs with Pop. He heard Pop's door close. He told himself that he was going to have to get used to stuff like this. She wasn't going out with Professor Mulvaney anymore. So it looked like Miz Bean was only fucking one man.

There was a package from Mr. O'Nolan. It was a book of pictures about the Battle of Gettysburg. You saw the picture of what the place looked like now and then you saw what it looked like after the actual battle. Some of the dead bodies were really Union soldiers wearing Confederate uniforms off corpses and making believe they'd been shot. There was a book from Miz Bean that was a complete set of plans for a monastary in France. Parts of it looked like parts of castles. It had all the details. There was an antique tool chest made of wood that he could keep his things in. There was a heavy hatchet for clearing his trail. There were shirts and the biggest pair of cleat-bottomed boots he ever saw. There was a sketch pad and a set of fifty fine-tip felt pens in every color.

He and Miz Bean gave Pop the suede sports jacket that would close. He gave Pop a shirt in Extra Large that Miz Bean had helped him find. He gave Miz Bean a pair of driving gloves made of soft brown leather. Pop gave her a sweater. It had little buttons and it was thick and white. She wore it all morning. She tried her gloves on. She was wearing them and the sweater when she gave Pop the flat envelope. He opened it and said, "Airplane tickets. For a trip? Are we taking a trip, Lizzie?"

"It's three tickets," Miz Bean said. "We can all go on this one if we decide to go."

"They're to New York," Pop said.

Petey said, "Cool."

Miz Bean said, "It's more in the line of a business trip than anything else. There's old business you might take care of," she told Pop.

He looked at her. He said, "Is that what this is about?"

Miz Bean lifted her chin. She did it exactly the way Pop did. She lit another cigarette. "You take care of old business before you take care of new business. If you can. Maybe you can."

"Go back and let her—"

"*Let* nothing. Go back and do it right."

"I did it right."

"Properly, then."

"This one you don't do properly," Pop said. "This one, you lie and steal and fight."

"I'm not suggesting you give anything *up*," Miz Bean said.

"I'll bet you're not."

"You're not referring to what happened to me," she said.

Pop was shaking his head. "No," he said. "No. I didn't mean to. I wouldn't. You know that. I just don't—why do you want to *risk* it all?"

"So you can get protection for Petey and O'Nolan and us. So you won't be afraid to do that. So if we win we can *keep* it all. Because she's a person too. All of those reasons."

"What if we lose, Lizzie?"

"You're a detective. You find things. Go back and find witnesses to—you know."

"I've got them," Pop said.

"So we'll win."

"Maybe. Maybe we'll lose. That lawyer scared hell out of me, Lizzie."

"But don't run away *scared.*"

"I want my *boy!*" Pop shouted. Petey thought Pop was crying. "I don't want visiting rights to my son. I don't want to hear things about him and not know what's going on. I—" Pop turned to him. Pop was in his pajamas and the itchy bathrobe and heavy white socks. The hair on his chest showed. Some of it was white. "Where did you go last night?"

Petey said, "Me?"

"Damned right. Where did you go?"

"Out?"

"What?"

"I went out, Pop."

"*Where?*"

Miz Bean was in her bathrobe. She wore the sweater open over it. She looked pretty and soft. She was shaking her head for Pop to see. He waved his hand at her to make her stop. She said, "No more."

"Oh, no?" Pop said.

"Please," she said.

Petey stuck his chin in the air like Miz Bean. When he did it Petey thought about how she imitated Pop doing it. So they all stood there with their chins in the air pointing at each other. The Christmas tree lights were on. Petey looked at them. They looked like the

George Washington Bridge when you're driving home from someplace. You're sleeping in the back and your parents are in the front seat arguing. Their chins are pointed in the air.

Miz Bean put her hands together in front of her like somebody who's praying. She said, "Please."

Pop nodded. He said, "Sorry, folks. I'm sorry. Sorry."

"Me too," Miz Bean said. "I really thought it was the right idea. I should have talked to you first. I really *do* think it's the right idea. But we're going to have to talk. This is what happens when you get used to making little diagnoses for people and telling them how to run their lives. You get a little casual."

Pop was rubbing his face with both hands.

They were quiet. Petey said, "I went outside, up the hill across the road."

"Weren't you cold?" Miz Bean asked.

He nodded.

She said, "You were just thinking about things, weren't you?"

He nodded.

"It's a tough time of year sometimes," she said.

He nodded.

She put a hand behind his neck. She was still wearing the tight brown driving gloves. He smelled the leather.

Pop said, "And you were hearing all this—all this shit on Christmas morning. You know what we were referring to?"

Petey shook his head.

Pop said, "You don't know?"

Petey shook his head.

Pop closed his eyes. He said, "*Damn,* Petey. Damn it." He hugged Petey. Miz Bean hugged them both.

She said, "What the hell, guys. Merry Christmas anyway."

Pop said, "Anyway."

Snow was coming down by then. A cornhead went by on a snowmobile. Pop was cooking bacon for their breakfast. Petey looked at the soldiers lying on the grass at Gettysburg. He tried to figure out which ones were dead.

The day after Christmas Lugene Winton telephoned. Miz Bean answered. When she said "Who?" it was Mr. O'Nolan who went stiff first. Pop looked at the telephone and took a step. Miz Bean said, "*Who* is that?" Then she said, "You can talk to him, honey, he's sitting right here. Ah. No, of course I wouldn't. I'll be happy to tell him. And the same to you. Bye-bye." Pop was back at the stove. He was wearing pajamas and turning sausages and shaking tomato juice for everyone to have in a bloody mary. They were having brunch on the day after Christmas. Miz Bean was wearing the itchy blue bathrobe that Petey's mother had given Pop. Petey was thinking how he was going to have to get good at this. Pop looked at Petey and Petey looked away. The look said: *I'd be having one hell of a good time if you would smile for me*. He knew that look. His mom used to use it on them. Miz Bean said, "Lugene Winton says Merry Christmas, Petey. She was too shy to talk to you."

"She said that, Miz Bean?"

"She didn't say quite that. I figured it out. It's true."

Mr. O'Nolan said, "Another heart broken, and you haven't eaten your breakfast yet."

"No, sir," Petey said. "But we don't need another one of those around here."

"Watch it," Pop said. He almost growled.

"I apologize," Petey said. "It's embarrassing, is all. People always calling up."

"Aren't they," Mr. O'Nolan said.

"I don't blame him," Miz Bean said.

"Blame him," Pop said. He ran his hand over Petey's head and held the hair. "Blame him. He could use a little blame."

"Not on *my* time," Miz Bean said. "Petey, do you think you could put some boots on and fetch us a little firewood? If you wouldn't mind?"

He knew she was helping him escape. He went into the living room for his boots. Halfway into the closet he heard Miz Bean say, "We don't need much more about blame, thank you."

"No," Pop said.

Then Mr. O'Nolan said, very low, "May I ask a question?"

Pop said, "Shoot."

"Excuse me for asking it. But I was truly puzzled. Why is it that your wife never suspected how separate you really were? By that, I ask: why did she not take precautions? Why did she not infer that you would run, taking Peter with you?"

Petey nodded his head while he laced up his boots.

Miz Bean said, "I'm sorry to say I know the answer. I think it's simple. She was in love."

"*I'm* sorry," Mr. O'Nolan said. "But I thought there were—two? Would she have been in love with them both?"

The spatula hit the frying pan. The hot fat flared. Miz Bean said, "Oh, well, I wouldn't know that. Though it's possible in something—I just don't know. What I meant was that she was in love with not being in love with her husband anymore. I'm sure of it. She was drunk with it."

Petey left the other boot unlaced. He went out fast. He smelled it before he saw it. He heard it before he smelled it. Or he heard it and smelled it at the same time. Then he did see it. There was a snowmobile up on their hill at the crest. It was idling. He smelled the kerosene. Then they lit it up. It was pretty much the same place he would sit at with Pop's gun. There wasn't any dumb-ass kid up there with his father's pistol. There was a big cross. It was really tall and it looked funny because its arms were too short. The wind was down so the smell of kerosene wasn't strong but it was there. The fire on the cross burned yellow and red. It was a little hard to see because the sky was bright. There was a lot of black smoke though. The burning sound was like kindling in the wood stove. It was like laundry flapping on their backyard clothesline in Brooklyn. The front door slammed out behind him. Pop called out, "Mother*fuckers!*" He went past Petey. He went straight up the hill. The cross smoked away. The snowmobile started up into gear and went away over the back side of their hill. His father went across the road and over the fence and straight up. His arms pumped. His head was down. His pajamas flapped over his skinny white ankles.

Petey watched him. He got to the top faster than Petey ever could get there. He stood there and looked down the other side. Even from the dooryard Petey could see his chest filling up and emptying. Pop's face was red and his lips were pulled back from his teeth. He fell down but only one knee touched the ground. He stood up. He looked at the cross. It was bigger than Pop was. He turned his side to it. He kicked out. He kicked out again. The fire was pretty much down but Pop was kicking through the fire onto the cross. He kicked again. He kicked it again and it fell over partway. He moved closer and kicked again and it fell into the snow. Pop fell down too. He stayed on his knees. He put both hands together in a scoop and he shoveled snow onto the cross. Then he stayed on his hands and knees and panted. Then he came down. He slid and he tripped. Miz Bean came out with a blanket for him. Petey watched her. She was going to learn something now.

Pop didn't look at her. He walked past her to the woodpile and picked up a log and threw it. He threw another one. "*Moth*erfuckers," he said. He kicked up a thinner log and pounded it on top of the pile. He kicked at the pile and snarled. His chest was humping up and down. He was covered with sweat. His belly showed under his pajamas. Miz Bean stood next to Petey. She held the blanket out. She looked like a mother next to the bathtub when the child comes out to get warm and dry. Pop walked up and down the porch. He made noises. He panted. He said, "Motherfucking *Nazis*."

Then he stopped. He shook his head and took a very deep breath. Petey said, "Okay," and Miz Bean took a step. Petey said, "You can do it now."

Pop looked up. "You guys all right?" he said.

Petey didn't answer. He went onto the snow on the lawn and picked up the firewood. He carried it back to the pile and stacked it so the pile was tight and solid and neat.

Miz Bean put the blanket around Pop. "How do you feel?"

He answered, "You understand what I was saying about this? That we can't call in the cops or the Bureau? You understand why I feel so stupid and angry? Because there's nothing I can do except load my piece and go out shooting them one at a time." He looked at Petey. "I forget," he said. "How much of this do you know about?"

Mr. O'Nolan said, "Don't do *that*. Well, you won't. Will you?"

Pop looked up. He was shivering. They all walked to the door where Mr. O'Nolan stood. He was holding it open for them. Petey thought they all must look like Mr. O'Nolan's guests.

Mr. O'Nolan said, "*Will* you?"

Inside they sat in the kitchen. They all pulled their chairs closer to the wood stove and sat in there. The grown-ups drank coffee instead of the vodka drinks Pop had made. Petey drank cocoa. Everyone shivered. Mr. O'Nolan poured the coffee. *He's our host,* Petey thought.

The telephone rang. Miz Bean said, "Maybe it's Lugene."

Pop said, "She wouldn't call a boy twice. Right, Petey?"

"Shy or bold, she wouldn't call twice," Petey said. "That's right."

On the fifth ring, Mr. O'Nolan said, "We know our caller, do we not?"

Everyone's head went up and down.

"So that we need not hear his message again," Mr. O'Nolan said.

Everybody shook their head.

"Then let's drink a bloody mary. You get tomato juice with celery salt, Peter, I'm afraid. Let us toast some patron saint of the day. Hermann Goering, perhaps? And let us salute the marvels of the physics of sound. You see? They ring and we fail to answer. And yet their message comes through." Mr. O'Nolan was handing around the big glasses with ice in them. Every time he passed a glass he said, "Cheers." They all kept trying to laugh.

On New Year's Eve Mr. O'Nolan babysat for his grandson. Pop and Miz Bean and Petey stayed home. They sat in the upstairs TV room and watched "Dick Clark's Rockin New Year's Eve." These wimpy singers with blond hair kept smiling. Petey was thinking about his mother. He wondered who she was with. Everybody got very happy or very sad on New Year's Eve. He hoped she was sad. He knew Pop was. Miz Bean didn't talk at first. Then she talked mostly to Petey. They made fun of the peoples' dancing. When he got quiet to watch a girl lean back and make her tits shake Miz Bean stared at him and made her eyebrows go up and down a few times. She said, "It's called sex."

Pop said, "What?"

"I knew it would get his attention," she said.

Petey laughed. "It got mine," he said. He was watching the girls. He was also thinking about Lugene. He wished he was old enough to get married. He also wished he would never have to think about it. The telephone rang. Pop looked up. He looked different. Miz Bean looked at the television set. Petey said, "It's them."

Pop said, "No."

"It's for you," Miz Bean said.

"It's for me? You think it's Lugene?"

"No," Pop said.

Miz Bean said, "Pick it up and say hello." She lit another cigarette. He remembered the diner. He remembered her office when she cried. Her voice sounded like that. "Use your head, Petey. Like the man always says."

He was terribly frightened. It was worse than the KKK. He wished it *was* the KKK. All they did was kick you and shoot you and burn crosses and burn down your house. This was something worse. He knew it. When he went out of the room Pop was sitting with his head back against the sofa and his eyes closed. He wished Pop would call him back. Miz Bean was trying to smile. He felt like someone at a station who was going away.

In Pop's bedroom the sheets were messy. Miz Bean's clothes were over the chair next to Pop's bureau. He was getting used to that. One way or another he might end up as Miz Bean's kid. He wished he could be. He wished he could have started out as her kid. He said, "Hello?"

Nobody talked to him. His stomach was cold. He felt sick. He felt his head going like a pulse. Then the phone scraped on something at the other end. She said, "It's Mommy. Darling, it's your *Mommy.*" She was crying. So was he. He figured all that would have to happen now was that Pop started in whimpering. "It's Mommy," she said.

He said, "How'd you find us, Mom?"

"Is *that* all you're worried about? How I found you? Petey, how *are* you? How am *I?* Don't you miss your *Mommy?*"

"Aw, Ma," he tried to say. He was crying too hard. He said, "Ma." He said, "Hi."

"Hi," she said. "I love you. I miss you. I didn't let you go away from me on purpose. Did you know that?"

He took a deep breath. "The other day."

"That's better than nothing," she said. "Happy birthday, Peter."

"It isn't my birthday, Mom."

"Birthday? Did I say that? I didn't mean to, darling. Happy New Year, I meant. I'm at a party. But I had to tell you—Petey?"

"Who told you what number to call, Mom?"

He heard her breathe into the phone. "Your father," she said. "He called me up at a number and I wasn't there. He started calling a lot of numbers and a lot of people and, you know, he *looked.* You know him. He finally found me. Petey, *I'd* been looking for *you!* All over! He called me and he told me. We arranged for me to call. I'll be there *soon.* I'm coming for you."

"*I'm a detective. I find things,*" Petey said in Pop's voice.

She giggled. She sounded like a girl in school. Petey

185

laughed too. She said, "All right? You can pack your stuff, darling."

"Is that all right with Pop?"

"It doesn't matter what's all right with anyone. You're my baby."

"But he's my father. You're my mom. Couldn't you—no."

"No," she said. "No." Then she said, "And there are other people, anyway."

"Miz Bean?"

"Is that her name? Miz Bean?"

"Are you—Jesus. Mom? Are you going with more than one guy?"

"There are people I see."

"Mom. I don't know how to do this."

"Will you call me, Petey? Your father has my numbers. Will you call me up?"

He nodded.

"Petey?"

He nodded.

"Petey!"

"Hi, Mom."

"Darling. *Call* me. Call me tomorrow or in a day or two. Will you?"

"Okay," Petey said.

"Aren't you *happy?*"

Petey nodded.

"Please?" she said.

"I missed you, Mom."

She was crying again. She said, "Thank you."

"What?"

"I love you."

"I love you, Mom."

"Call me up, darling. Bye-bye."

"Should I put Pop on?"

"Tell him it was me."

"He knows."

"Yes," she said. "Say hello for me."

They said they loved each other. They said goodbye. Petey blew his nose on a tissue that smelled like Miz Bean's perfume. His head felt as big as the bed. He carried it on his shoulders very carefully because it was going to break. He sat on the bed. He held his head so it wouldn't fall. He tried to think how it happened. He remembered what Pop had said to Miz Bean and Mr. O'Nolan. Pop was getting them all in trouble because he was afraid to call the cops, he had said. He was afraid to call them because they would let the word get back to Mom. He should know about those things, Petey figured. If word got back then Mom would come and get him. But Pop hadn't called the cops or the FBI. Petey knew that. They would have come and talked to everybody. So if he hadn't given in and called the FBI and the cops then why had he called up Mom? *I'm a detective, I find things.* Petey remembered the tickets for them to fly to New York that Miz Bean had given Pop. She wanted Pop to tell Mom where they were. That would mean they were aboveboard. But that meant she could be with Pop while he was aboveboard. It didn't mean she would have to be with Petey. He knew from Pop that Mom would come and take him back. So maybe she was trying to get that to happen so she could be alone with Pop. That meant Miz Bean was trying to get rid of him. That couldn't be. So it had to be that *Pop* was trying to get rid of him. But that couldn't be either.

Pop was straight with him. He was fucking Miz Bean
anyway whether or not Petey was there. Petey looked
at the sheets and rubbed his balls. He took his hand
away. He felt like he was stealing from them. He
looked away from the sheets.

He sat like that. Pop came in. He said, "You all
right?"

Petey tried to nod. His head hurt too much.

"You know why I called her?"

Petey tried to shake his head.

Pop talked anyway. "I can't think of a reason. I want
you to live here all the time with me. You're my kid.
You used to be my baby. You're my kid. How much
about how we ended up here do you know?"

Petey talked with his lips stiff. He heard himself.
He sounded like somebody with a split lip. "I heard
you tell Mr. O'Nolan."

"Geez. You know it all. You know too *much*. I said
some rough things, Petey. I was mad."

"Surprise," Petey said.

Pop tried to smile. "Lizzie thought I should tell your
mother. She got me thinking that way. Anyhow, I'm
probably going to have to call the state guys and the
Bureau. These assholes around here. Excuse me. But
you know."

"Except you want to try and do it yourself."

Pop said, "You know the worst of me, don't you? I
don't have a brother except for you. You're probably
the closest thing to a brother I have except for O'Nolan. But you come first there. Brother *and* son. And
I'm tempted to load up and go after those guys. But
that's crazy. I should call the cops. I'm worried about
you and O'Nolan and Lizzie."

"Except," Petey said.

Pop said, "Yeah. I was thinking about taking the whole thing my own way. And then I was thinking about calling in the real cops and letting them do it. Except either way, I figured, I could end up losing you." Pop's face looked soft. Petey wiped at his own eyes with Miz Bean's tissue.

Petey said, "So why'd you call Mom up?"

His father turned his face. He looked like a big dog looking at something new. "You don't *know*?"

"I don't know nothing, Pop."

"So you could be with your *mother*."

"That's it? You mean you did this whole thing for me?"

Pop shouted so loud the windows made noises. His face was red. He kicked at a wicker chair and it sailed across the room. Petey jumped. Pop shouted again. "Who the fuck else would I break my fucking heart for like this?"

Petey lowered his face down into his hands. He couldn't help it. He kept on crying even when Pop came over and kneeled down next to him and squeezed him hard and stayed there. Petey didn't think he would stop. He did remember how. He stopped.

They stayed up later than he did. They made him go to bed early. He was thinking of it. He was really thinking about going up onto the hill. But they made him get into bed. He fell asleep listening to them talk. He didn't hear the words. He felt sick. It was like being very sick and listening to people talk about how sick you were but you couldn't hear the words.

When he got up there was bacon frying and coffee

and eggs. Pop and Miz Bean talked and talked. He listened. He didn't have anything to say back. He wanted to. He didn't want to sulk. He kept trying to say things because they were working so hard. They moved the big TV set downstairs. Pop went up onto the ice and snow on the roof and snaked the antenna cable to the living room window. He got it open and shoved the cable through. They hooked it up. Miz Bean said it was so they could all watch the New Year's Day games together. He didn't think she liked football. She was working for him. That made him feel worse about not thinking of anything to say.

He hated the people on the teams. They jumped around and walked around and waved their hands in the air. They acted like everything they did mattered. It only mattered to the jerks in the stands. It didn't matter to Petey. He knew it didn't matter to Pop or Miz Bean. They were watching him. He decided to root for Penn State because their uniforms were black.

They ate lunch in the living room. They walked around outside together. Everyplace he went they made up reasons for being there with him. They watched more games. He kept falling asleep. It was like having a fever. He tried to make believe he wasn't sleeping but he kept on falling asleep. When he woke up nobody acted like he'd been sleeping with his mouth open and saliva on his lips. They ate dinner in the living room while they watched a game. Miz Bean kept falling asleep. When she wasn't asleep she was yawning. Pop didn't say much. He watched them and he didn't talk either after a while. It was Miz Bean who did most of the talking. But she was yawning all the time. She was pale. He wondered if she was sick too. They made him go to bed early. They hugged him and they watched him go upstairs. He felt really bad for them. But he was sick and there was nothing he could do. He fell asleep and had terrible dreams. He couldn't remember them in the morning. All weekend he tried to remember them. He thought maybe if he told Miz Bean it would give them something to talk about. But he couldn't remember any of the dreams. All weekend while he tried to remember and to think of something to say they watched him and stayed with him. Everybody acted like they all were sick.

On Monday morning Miz Bean carried a suitcase to her car. Before she got in she hugged Pop. She hugged Petey. She had tears in her eyes. It was like everybody going in different directions at LaGuardia. But they all went to school. They saw her car in the parking lot. They didn't say anything about it. They hadn't said anything all the way in.

Pop went up to the guidance suite. Petey went to his locker. Lugene Winton was there. Her face was shining. She said good morning. He looked at her. Then he remembered he was supposed to be grateful because she left a Merry Christmas message. He was supposed to be excited. He didn't know what to say. He watched her eyes. He said, "Merry Christmas, Lugene." She looked at him. He waited. She was wearing a purple sweater and really tight jeans. Her face turned into one of those faces you make when you find out there's barf on your cafeteria table. He was maybe going to say, *My mother called*. Probably he wasn't. She walked away.

He saw DiStefano near the library doors. When he walked over DiStefano held his finger out. "Smell it," he said.

"Eat it," Petey said.

"It's your friend Lugene. I thought maybe you'd like a sniff." Petey hit DiStefano across the mouth with his math book. DiStefano stood and looked at him.

Petey said, "Yuh want I should swat yuh one maw time?" Petey heard himself sound like Brooklyn. He loved it. All the guys who used to beat him up sounded like that. Petey was smiling so hard that DiStefano was looking at his mouth. Petey figured DiStefano was confused. He liked that. *My mom called up.*

Inside the library there were loud voices. He heard them through the closed doors. When he opened one he said, "That's him." Petey could see him from the back. He was wearing heavy pants and a black and red checked shirt and khaki suspenders. He was in snow-mobile boots and an orange hunting hat. He was shouting at Miz Demeter. Petey knew it was him.

The Reverend Staynes was saying, "I do not care if you call this a library challenge. You want to say challenge, girlie, you got *challenge*. I herewith challenge your right to keep this kind of Negro filth, unChristian filth, homosexual filth on the shelves I happen to pay my taxes on."

"You *do* hold down a job?" Miz Demeter said. She was shaking. Her voice was shaking too.

Petey told DiStefano, "You go get my father and bring him down here. You don't come back with him, I'm gonna clean yuh clock with a wide variety of text-books. Yuh heah me?"

DiStefano looked at him and then he went. He kept

shaking his head. Miz Demeter was saying, "There is a committee made up of board members and admin- istrators and instructional staff as well as myself. We make the decisions according to a well-defined policy about what we want on our shelves."

Reverend Staynes stepped toward her. Miz Deme- ter stepped back. One of the library clerks had her mouth in an O-shape in her round fat face. She looked like a doughnut with a hole. Petey laughed but made himself stop. Reverend Staynes held out a piece of paper. "I got thirty-six signatures here—"

"It's wonderful that all of you can write," Miz Dem- eter said.

"Don't come on mighty with me, girlie. Only Christ the Lord is mighty. The rest of us, supposed to render up to Caesar what is Caesar's and to God what belongs to *Him*. What we are *talking* about here is pure blas- phemy—listen! 'Her moans gave way to sobs and cries' it says in this precious *Another Country* you just have to have in your precious library. Same place as it has that sex it says '*I woke up this morning with my mind/Stayed on Jesus!*' Comes within sixty, sixty-five pages of the lewdness the likes of which a grown man can't imagine. Miscegenation of the races *contra* God's law, meaning Ishmaelites and children of the Lord mating in all their sweat and lust and cries of base appetite in their differing colors of skin. In the self- same breath, near as to the number, as the name of Jesus Lord and Savior is invoked, never *mind* it's in the accent of the Negro who God ordains to be sepa- rate and just purely *not* the equal of the white. I'm telling you Constitution of the United States, girlie. You see them equal in there? Is that what the Founding Fathers wanted? It is not. Three-fifths the same as others. It says so in the book. And your black man's book says 'bitch,' says 'shit' and some words I guarantee you couldn't understand unless you served in the service under the Constitution this here is *violating* seven ways from Sunday and back. Three *fifths!* We want it off. Outside the school. Away from our children. And burned if possible in public *locus*. You listening to me, girlie?"

Miz Demeter was back against a library table. Her hair was all over. She pushed it with both her hands. She said, "If you're a student or a teacher or a book, you may stay. If you wish to return the James Baldwin novel that someone filched and that you hold in your hand, please do so. In fact, *please* do so. Then leave."

Pop was next to him. He patted Petey on the bottom. He walked into the library. He was on his toes. Petey was grinning. The grin got wider. Pop stood behind the Reverend Staynes. He spread his legs a little then got onto his toes. Then he put his leg behind the Reverend Staynes so it was in back of both of his legs. He put his hand above the Reverend Staynes's head. He grabbed hold of his hair and pulled back. The Reverend Staynes screamed like a bird. Petey laughed the biggest laugh of the month. Miz Demeter said, "Drop in." Then she put her hand over her mouth and laughed too. Pop pulled the Reverend Staynes by his hair. His heels banged on the floor. His boots made a bouncing sound. Pop shifted to the Reverend Staynes's shirt collar but kept the top part of his body when he pulled. That was because he was dragging him so fast.

"Against the law!" the Reverend Staynes shouted.

Kids were in the hall watching. Some of them followed. Petey did. Teachers put their heads out of doorways to watch. After a while they were lined up in the corridor.

"Intervention in citizen justice," the Reverend Staynes shouted.

"Police brutality," DiStefano suggested.

"All *right!*" some cornhead agreed.

Somebody else yelled, "Pearl Harbor!"

"This school is filled with assholes," Petey shouted.

"Habeas corpus!" the Reverend Staynes called.

Pop dragged him down the steps to the side door. The boots bounced like drums. Then Pop dropped Reverend Staynes and pushed the door open. Pop said, "Out. I *ever* see you again. I ever get a *message* from you—you're the one, aren't you? There couldn't be two of you, could there? I ever even hear a *rumor* about you, I'm coming up. I'm armed, day and night." Petey wanted to sit down and worry about it. He hoped Pop was lying. The gun ought to be in the roasting pan. "I'm coming up to see you. I'll put a shot into your elbow, one shot into each elbow bone, you shithead. You'll have to zip your fly up with your teeth and your tongue. Understand? I'm a cop. I can shoot *pieces* off of you. Understand?"

He's a detective. He finds things.

The Reverend Staynes didn't answer. He stood up. Pop stepped on the back of his knee and his leg caved in. He fell down again. He crawled a little distance away. Then he stood up again. He looked at Pop. Pop was waiting to do something else. The Reverend

Staynes's face was very white. It didn't look like a face. It looked like an elbow or a knee. There wasn't anybody on it. Petey looked over to Pop. When Pop moved the Reverend Staynes walked out. He walked slowly. Pop pulled the door closed behind him. Everybody in the hall waited. Then they started to clap. Petey did too. He thought that it was like being on one of those teams on New Year's Day. All *right!*

It got hot the next day. Everything melted a little bit. Miz Bean called it a meltdown. Everybody knew it would freeze up that night. All of a sudden it was forty-one degrees and cornheads were taking their shirts off in the parking lot near the bus stops. Girls wore tee-shirts. DiStefano talked about everybody's tits. Petey looked at them all. Pop wore a bow tie and a purple shirt and the sports jacket that closed. He might have been wearing the gun too because Petey couldn't find it in the roasting pan in the pantry. He thought if he needed it he would look in the bedroom. Maybe Pop had started keeping it in the bedroom. He wondered just what he meant by needing it. Pop came to school looking like a policeman in disguise. Miz Bean wore a heavy sweater and told everybody it would freeze soon. Mr. Zacharias told her she was a party pooper. Mr. Staschauer told her she was a Cassandra. All the men hung around her. Petey wondered if they knew his mother was coming to get him. He wondered what she would say. He wondered if Miz Bean would hang around when it happened. He thought probably she'd go someplace and be by herself and smoke cigarettes. He knew that she was like him.

After school Mr. O'Nolan was waiting for them at home. He was dressed up too. He looked like he belonged in his sports jacket. Pop looked like he had borrowed his even if it did close over the belly. Mr. O'Nolan looked dapper. He smiled with his sad face. Miz Bean drove up in the BMW. They heard her outside. She clanked. She came in with a bottle of gin and a long bottle of tonic water. She had limes. She told them it was the first gin and tonic party of the new year in honor of a meltdown. She had root beer for Petey. She made drinks for the rest of them. They sat in the kitchen. Pop had the fire going because the house was damp and chilly. They drank gin and tonics. Pop and Mr. O'Nolan were getting excited about history again. They were talking about Nigger Holler. Mr. O'Nolan was figuring out for Pop where Pop should go in New York City to look for information about the Underground Railroad. Petey figured they'd be using the tickets Miz Bean had given Pop for Christmas. He figured that meant his mother wouldn't take him away alone. They'd all fly into New York together. Then Pop would give him up. He wondered if Miz Bean would hang around for that. She probably wouldn't want to. He wished that she would. It would be better if she would. Pop and Mr. O'Nolan were getting very excited. Pop said, "Why don't you come with me?"

"Well. I confess that I hadn't considered it. I thought of the project as exclusively yours."

"I don't care whose project it is. Come in with me and let's eat clams at the Oyster Bar in Grand Central. We can roll some junkies in Bryant Park, behind the library. We could eat in places down in Chinatown you never heard of. Or Little Italy? We could see—what would you want to see? A movie? Some kind of musical? On me."

"I would love to see *Noises Off*. The British comedy?"

"All right," Pop said.

"Or the opera," Mr. O'Nolan said. "The Met's doing *Otello*."

"Okay," Pop said. "The opera. You know how to get tickets?"

"You've never been?"

"It always sounded a little rich for my blood. And a little smart. And slightly phony, to tell you the truth."

"I'm a fool about music," Mr. O'Nolan said. "I should say, a fool *for* music. I love it. I could sit down now and drink a gin and tonic too many and listen to—name it. Heavy metal rock 'n' roll or Edward Elgar's least little, I don't know: say his *Falstaff*. Mantovani and the Thousand and One Strings playing elevator music. I confess. But I'm also a fool *about* music. I don't know very much. I can't remember the names of most of the operas, much less their plot or structure. But when the hall is dark, I don't care if it's New York or Salt City Playhouse in Syracuse, and the soprano begins to sing, I weep. I start right away. As if it all is about—something else. I suspect that most opera *is* about something else. Would you care to try it?"

"Even if I never went? Do we need to rent tuxedos?"

Mr. O'Nolan reached across the table. He patted the back of Pop's hand. He shook his head. He smiled the nicest smile. Petey closed his eyes a minute. He knew he'd never get to go there with them or talk to them when they came back from it. He really wanted to. He wanted to see Pop that happy. Pop was only happy with Miz Bean and Mr. O'Nolan and him. When he was with Mr. O'Nolan it was like Pop already had his master's degree. It was like people telling him he was already a teacher.

Miz Bean pulled Petey's hand. She walked into the living room and started to put her boots on. She pointed at Petey's boots. He sat on the floor and put them on too. She called to the kitchen, "We're going for a walk, gents. We'll be careful of low-flying fascists. We'll be back soon." They got their coats on but left the gloves and hats because it still was warm at four-thirty in the afternoon. Outside, Petey smelled the snow that was coming. Clouds were lining up over their hill.

Miz Bean said, "Show me your trail, would you, Petey? Or is it too private?"

"I made it so people could get down there," he said.

"But then you used it for *you* to get down. Because it's private down there. Didn't you build yourself a fort?"

He said, "It's for people to use to get down there."

"Then I'd like it if we went there."

The snow was very deep and the hill became steep. They had to hold each other's hand sometimes. He was afraid Miz Bean would fall if he didn't hold onto her. It didn't feel like a mother's hand. If she and Pop got married it still wouldn't feel like a mother's hand. It was like a girl's hand. It was scary holding on to it. It felt very good. He was sure he was blushing. Her hand was strong. Sometimes it didn't feel like he was helping her. Sometimes it felt like Miz Bean was doing the helping.

At the wood bridge she stood still. She was catching her breath and brushing snow off. She said, "You built that? Alone?"

Petey said, "It's like an early Roman bridge, isn't it? I think it's like a bridge they made in England where the Thames was narrow. Before they got around to making it out of stone. They'd do logs to get the patrols across. Then they'd do stone when they had time." He jumped down to it and kicked snow away from the bottom. "You can see where I started laying in the rocks for support."

"You made them in an *arch*."

"Oh, sure. This gully fills up with water in the spring, so you have to have someplace for it all to flow. It really runs, you know?"

"How did you learn that you should do that, Petey?"

"Books," he said. "I mean, books and also you just have to use your head. It all just makes sense."

"You enjoy this, showing off to your father's girl-friend?" She was smiling a big smile. His face felt hot enough to melt the snow.

"I wish you were *my* girlfriend!" He laughed to show her it was a joke. He heard the noise he'd made. It was like somebody screaming with a broken leg.

She came over to him and kissed him on the cheek. She hugged his neck. "I'm more of a girlfriend than anything else," she said. "I'm your friend, and I'm your father's friend. I'm *always* your friend. Like an old sister. Okay? Anytime you want. Any time."

"You mean, after."

She nodded her head.

He wanted to kiss her and hug her back. He wanted to get inside her coat with her and stay there and fall asleep. He said, "You still have to see the fort."

She moved her hand. He thought she was going to hold his hand. He stepped ahead of her. He didn't know why. She followed. The snow was up to their knees in some places. So he kicked it as he walked to make a trail for her. There was a little bit of light. The snow looked dark. It was heavy. The trees were crowded in together. The sun was going down. When they came to the fort it looked like a dark lump of snow. All the stones of the walls and the two-by-fours that framed the door and the poles of the roof were covered with wet snow on top of ice. He kicked some away. She told him how brilliant it was. He pulled the two-by-four away that propped the door shut. The door was made of one-by-tens. He was going to put brass hinges on the frame some time. He didn't invite Miz Bean in. He got onto his knees and crawled inside. She came after him.

It was ice cold. It was completely dark. It smelled like wet wood. He pushed back until he sat against a wall. His hands were cold now. His stomach was jumping. Miz Bean was sitting to his right against another wall. She had her legs folded in front of her. He could feel her knee with his knee. They sat.

"You come down here," she said.

"Sometimes," he said. "I did in the warm weather."

"You feel safer down here?"

"I—uhm. This is—older kids aren't supposed to, you know. This is where I play."

"Games, you mean?"

He could smell her mouth and her perfume. "I can talk out loud. I make things up."

"Knights?"

He nodded. He knew she couldn't see him but he nodded.

She said, "Killing and hacking and shields clanging, that kind of thing?"

He nodded. It felt to him like she knew what he was thinking whether he said anything or not.

"Any princesses or queens?"

"No. Sometimes."

"But mostly it's alone," she said.

He nodded *yes*.

It was still dark. It was always dark. It was the place where they couldn't see you. He was thinking how well he had chinked the poles and rocks with daub and moss. He heard her coat move. She was hugging his neck. Her face was wet. She kissed him on his nose. She kissed his mouth. He thought for a second that this was a girlfriend kiss. His heart slammed his chest and it hurt. But it was closer to a mother kiss. But it was on his mouth. She said, "I love you. Understand?"

Yes.

She crawled out of his fort. He could hear her clothes move. He crawled after her. He didn't think about staying behind. But she said, "Come on, Petey. Come with me." They stood up in the snow and brushed the snow and ice and dirt off their clothes. "I thought I heard them calling us," Miz Bean said. It was almost dark. It was dark enough. She said, "Did you hear that?"

They stood still and listened. Somebody shouted. It

sounded like the Indian whoops in an old John Wayne movie. There was only one, though. Then there was another.

Then Petey remembered. "It sounds like the Civil War," he said. "In the movies. The rebs make that sound."

Miz Bean said, "Oh, my God. The factory shift's let out. The gas stations are closed. The boys are home from work and they're *attacking*."

Petey said, "Attacking?"

"I don't know what they're doing. But aren't they the ones who burned the cross? Don't you think that's—somebody saw him and reported the black man was back and they're—I don't know. I don't know. Petey? We should get back. Really. Yes?"

"Yes, ma'am," he said.

Her head whipped around. She looked at him with her eyes staring. "What?" she said.

He said, "I said 'Yes, ma'am.'"

"Oh. Yes, *ma'am*. I didn't hear you right. I thought you said *mom*. I didn't hear you right."

"Yes," Petey said.

She looked away. "Right," Petey heard her say. "Right."

She started up the trail. Petey followed behind. Sometimes she stuck her hand out for him. He took it.

Whenever his mother came it would be sad. Everyone would be crying or trying not to cry. He and his mother would drive away after everybody had talked. Pop would probably be happy to see him go because it would be so uncomfortable around his mom. Miz Bean would write to him later on and tell him that he shouldn't feel bad. She would say to Pop, "Petey knows you love him." That would be true. But that doesn't make people feel better. Being loved by somebody is sometimes only as good as not being shot by somebody. Petey decided to tell this. He thought about telling Miz Bean. He would say, "There is all kinds of misery." He felt bad about not thinking to tell his mom. He wondered how you could want to hang around somebody who wasn't your mother or your girlfriend but who you felt both ways about. There *is* all kinds. He wondered where his mother would take him. He would have to start a new school again. It would be like with the cornheads. You walked into the room and they all turned around to watch you walk in.

He stood still for a second. He remembered how much he'd forgotten to worry about. Pop and Mr. O'Nolan were up there with probably the cornhead KKK. And all he could think about was selfish problems and how much he wanted to stay here. He thought that what he wanted was to know that Miz Bean was up at the house calling down to them. He and Pop would be on his trail. They would be down past the fort where the trail ended. The blacker forest would be there. They would be deciding whether to walk into it and trespass and look around. Petey would tell Pop he had never gone there. He'd tell how he was scared to. They would laugh. Or they would just take a breath and walk in. Mr. O'Nolan would be up at the house with Miz Bean. Miz Bean would call from the house and they'd turn back. It wasn't easy. You could never decide a thing like that. Nobody should ask you to make a choice between your mother and your father. Nobody should ask your father to make a choice between you and himself.

Petey was holding Miz Bean's hand. He stopped and so did she. "What?" she said.

Petey wanted to say what he just had learned. You can't *make* the choice. You can't. So it was like not having to do it. If you couldn't make it then you didn't have to. All you had to do was wait and see. All you had to do was be careful to not make up your mind.

He said, "We better hurry up."

They were breathing hard. The light was pretty much gone. The wet snow and melting slush were setting up because the cold was coming. They walked through the snow on top of the dead garden. Their feet were wet and so were their pants. Miz Bean's hand felt very cold. He pulled on it.

She said, "Is it something? All right? Are we—"

"Could I go ahead of you, please?"

She squeezed his hand. He led her. They tiptoed in snow across the side yard. At the side door they stood still. They heard the Reverend Staynes. Petey hoped the cellar door was still open. He turned the knob and pulled on the door and it opened out without a sound. He heard Miz Bean breathe hard behind him. "*Nigger!*" was a word he heard through the trees and around the corner of the house. He heard it again. "Nigger." They went in.

Miz Bean was holding onto his coat. He thought of elephants going down Flatbush Avenue once when a circus came. They held onto the tail of the elephant in front. She held onto him. The cellar smelled like water and oil. It smelled old. They bumped into boxes and posts. They went to the steps and up. He knew the door would be locked from the inside of the bathroom. He put one hand on the banister and one hand on the wall of the landing. He lifted up and kicked the door with both feet. He kept lifting and kicking. The latch on the other side of the bathroom door popped off. He heard it clang onto the floor. They went through.

Before they left the bathroom he tried to tell Miz Bean what to do. He couldn't. He didn't have enough air in his chest. His heart was making noises. She touched his shoulders. He stepped back. He wanted to breathe. She said, "Are you all right?"

He nodded. *Yes.*

She said, "I'm going to call the State Police. Do you want to stay here?"

He blew the air out. He said, "You go ahead. I'll be right there." He breathed some more. Then he said, "You better stay inside."

Miz Bean said, "*We* better stay inside. I'll use the phone upstairs."

They went up together. She went to the big bedroom. Petey thought of it as her and Pop's room. Probably it was. He went to his own room. He went for the underwear drawer. Then he went downstairs. He could hear Miz Bean talking.

Petey went into the kitchen. He crawled so they wouldn't see him through the front window. He crawled into the pantry but he came walking back. He didn't care just then if they saw him or not. He ran upstairs. He went into their room. Miz Bean was still talking very low into the phone. He looked under pillows. He pulled drawers out of the bureau and onto the floor. Miz Bean was looking at him. He figured she was thinking about the library. He tried to smile to reassure her. He didn't think it was working. But he got lucky soon enough on the second shelf of his father's bedside table under a copy of *Newsweek*. He went downstairs and into the bathroom and down into the cellar. When he came up out of the cellarway he went around the corner of the house. He went wide so they wouldn't see him coming. He was in the road. He stopped and checked the drum. This time it was full. It felt heavier because it was full. It scared him as much as anything. He was walking the same way he had come the night he'd tried to run away. It was when the hunters had kicked his leg so hard. He thought his leg was beginning to hurt again. He stopped. He got everything ready. Then he went the last part.

There were two black snowmobiles. Their engines were off. The Reverend Staynes was standing on one. He looked like a real preacher up there. He was wearing a white sheet. It was over a coat so he looked a little fatter. He had the hood on. He looked like Hallowe'en. His snowmobile boots stuck out at the bottom. There was a big guy with a sheet and hood and there was a little guy with a sheet and hood. He recognized the hook. There were six or seven people behind them in the road. Two of them must have been midgets or kids. They all stood there and looked out of these eyeholes. Petey tried to laugh. He sounded to himself like a horse getting really irritated. Three people had guns. The little hunter was pointing his rifle at Pop and Mr. O'Nolan. He moved the hook and it smoked. Then he lifted it and puffed through a mouth hole in the hood.

The Reverend Staynes saw him. "There!" he

shouted. Pop and Mr. O'Nolan turned. Mr. O'Nolan walked toward Petey. Pop put a hand on Mr. O'Nolan's shoulder. He and Pop looked like a couple of salesmen all dressed up to sell things to the cornheads. Mr. O'Nolan was shivering. Petey looked again. Pop was too. He heard the big hunter's voice though none of the hoods moved. It said, "It's the nigger's kid."

"I would be proud," Mr. O'Nolan said. "Be careful, Petey."

Pop said, "I'd be proud too."

Mr. O'Nolan giggled. He sounded peculiar. The Reverend Staynes called out, "He is armed! He is *armed!*"

They were looking at him. Petey remembered. It all went away from him. He couldn't hear them anymore. He could see. He couldn't hear them. He was moving.

He skidded on the snow. He had been running and then he slid toward them with his legs apart. The pistol was up in the air. The pistol was high and in his hand. He slid at them down the road. The big hunter was starting to move his rifle. Mr. O'Nolan was shouting at Petey. He could see his teeth and tongue. The big hunter's rifle moved. The little hunter's rifle pointed at Pop and Mr. O'Nolan. Pop held onto Mr. O'Nolan's shoulder. Mr. O'Nolan didn't move. Petey wanted to watch his father's face. He couldn't see it. It was there but he couldn't tell what was on it. Mr. O'Nolan lifted both hands into the air. Petey thought he looked like he was crying. He looked at Pop. He could tell that he wasn't crying. His face was red and his teeth were all over the front of it. Petey was glad to see it again. The two rifles kept moving. Petey skidded toward them and stopped.

The Reverend Staynes pointed at him. That made him fall off the snowmobile. The small hunter started to laugh. Petey saw the hood shake. He pushed the hood back and Petey saw that his teeth were crooked on top with a lot of the ones on the bottom missing. But he wasn't laughing at the Reverend Staynes. The Reverend Staynes's feet were on the long saddle of the snowmobile. The rest of him was behind it. But the little hunter was pointing at Petey and laughing at Petey.

Petey stood in front of them. Pop's gun was in his hand. The barrel was against his forehead. The guys in the sheets started to laugh when he put the barrel in his mouth. He took it out when he couldn't talk that way. He pushed the barrel against his head so it hurt. He was doing it. Some things you don't decide. That was what he was doing. He was standing in front of the cornhead KKK and his father and his father's best friend Mr. O'Nolan. He was screaming at them, "Stop it! Stop it! Stop it!" He could hear himself and everything else now.

Miz Bean at the front door was screaming too. She called, "Petey! *Please!*"

The big hunter's gun was coming up. His high voice was laughing like hell. The little hunter was laughing too. Mr. O'Nolan said, "Peter. Peter. My boy—"

"He *is* the nigger's kid," the little hunter said.

The Reverend Staynes was up and holding onto the snowmobile. He said, "All the more reason. *Pro bonum.* All the more."

Pop said, "He's mine. He's mine."

Petey closed his eyes. He opened them. He held the grip hard. He moved the gun away from himself. It wasn't about him now. He didn't need to spin the cylinder this time. He looked and looked, then he squeezed.

IT TOOK A long time for the State Police and the Sheriff's Department to find them. Once they came they never turned their lights off. Everything got shaken and beaten and thumped by the sirens. He couldn't hear because of the shot. He didn't remember that a shot sounded that loud. Sometimes he did hear and sometimes he couldn't. He could hear Pop tell a trooper that he sure did take his time. He heard Mr. O'Nolan tell Pop to shut up. He heard the trooper say that it was a good idea. Miz Bean didn't say anything that he could hear. He didn't say anything either.

The Reverend Staynes had gone over backwards again. But he had gone all the way around and over. He didn't just fall. First his leg above the knee opened up. It looked like a tomato all of a sudden. It got bigger before he fell. Then his legs had begun spinning. They spun under him and over. His legs were where his head should have been. His head was on the ground. It looked like he was standing on his head. He kept going over, though. So he ended up feet-first toward Petey. The blood kept coming out of his leg. He tried to reach it but he couldn't move that much. He fell back. He had kept crawling no place on his back. His hands and legs and face kept moving. He wriggled and squirmed. He kept saying, "Ah." He said it over and over.

Petey still held the gun out. He thought he'd cried, "I *missed!*" But he didn't know. The big hunter and the little hunter hadn't paused. They'd climbed onto the snowmobiles and they'd looked at Petey with the gun. Petey looked at the pistol too. Pop was running toward the hunters. Petey knew that Pop was coming to save him. They still had guns and Pop was running at them. Petey and the hunters looked. Pop shouted. Everyone looked up from looking at the Reverend Staynes. Pop scooped up a handful of snow and threw it at the hunters. He almost fell over. All the little cornhead people in the sheets began to run. Even one of them with a rifle began to run. They all ran down the Sergeant Magby Road toward the Faith and Beholden Tabernacle, Petey figured. Mr. O'Nolan and Miz Bean were laughing. Pop was in the snow next to the Reverend Staynes. The snowmobiles were gone by the time he'd stood up. Mr. O'Nolan reached out for the revolver. Petey laid it onto his hand. Miz Bean and Pop were bending over the Reverend Staynes. They were putting Pop's belt around his leg. He kept moving on the snow. He said, "Ah." Miz Bean put her coat on top of him. Pop came over to Petey. He said, "I'm sorry."

Miz Bean had wanted to carry the Reverend Staynes inside. Pop said No. Miz Bean said, "He could go into shock. He will. I think he *is*."

"Fuck him," Pop had said. "He'd have shot up half the house and several of us. Fuck him."

"If he dies, then Petey—"

"It was self-defense," Pop said. "It was self-defense." He walked over to the Reverend Staynes. He was yellow. He was getting gray. "Fuck him," Pop had said. He'd looked down. "Maybe just into the hall." Everybody picked the Reverend Staynes up except Petey. He'd stayed in the snow. He sat there. He stopped hearing for a while.

Later he'd felt Mr. O'Nolan shaking his shoulder. Petey had said, "I'm asleep." He was lying on the snow. He felt sleepy. He saw Mr. O'Nolan moving his mouth. Petey had said, "I stopped hearing again."

Now he was inside of the house. He'd started to hear when the sirens came and when the ambulance had left. Troopers kept coming over. Pop stood in front of him and crossed his arms. Petey could see his clothes bulge in the back. His father still had big muscles.

A cop said, "What was the victim's name again?"

Mr. O'Nolan said, "Staynes. The Reverend Staynes."

The cop said, "He sure as hell did have a lot of stains on him. *Stains?*"

Pop said, "Let me try and understand that one. Tell me if I get it right. Okay? You said stains, right? You were making a joke? About the guy's name? Stains, for Staynes?"

Miz Bean sounded mean too. She said, "That's awfully clever. Wordplay is so underrated in investigations of attempted lynchings and other rural violence. Don't you think?"

Mr. O'Nolan also sounded cruel. Petey had never heard him even angry. He figured they all were pretty pissed off about things. Mr. O'Nolan said, "Do you think he intends a *double entendre*? Is he making a pun about bloodstains?"

Miz Bean said, "Gosh. I wonder. Do you think it could be?"

"It was self-defense," Pop said.

Miz Bean said right away, "It always was."

Petey stopped hearing again. He stopped seeing. He figured he was falling asleep. When he got up it was darker and all the lights were on. Cops were still there. Everybody was drinking coffee. Pop was drinking whiskey. He was looking at Petey. Then he looked over his shoulder at the others. He looked nervous. He smelled bad from sweat. "It was self-defense," Pop said.

Petey heard Miz Bean say, "*Tell* him. Keep him and *tell* him that's what you're going to do."

Pop said, "Do you think we could talk about this upstairs or someplace?"

"No," she said. "Now. Tell him."

A cop said, "You folks can go right ahead and talk to each other. You say something I never heard before, I'll raise my hand, right? We're gonna stay here and we're gonna talk to the boy. Then we might have to ask him to accompany us to the barracks."

"County building," another cop said.

Pop stood up and turned around. He was on the

balls of his feet. Petey thought some cops might be in danger. Pop said, "You discuss fucking jurisdictions outside my house, all right? You discuss everything outside my house. You sons of bitches."

A cop said, "Hey, I'm sorry we got so riled up just because your son lays a man's body open with a .38 service revolver you always took such good care of."

The house got quiet. Mr. O'Nolan said, "Peter. We are standing by you. Is that clear?"

He heard Miz Bean say, "You *keep* him."

Pop said, "Don't you think I want to? Hey! Who gave me three tickets to New York for my fucking *Christmas* present?"

"I was wrong. I was trying to be right. I was having my famous scruples. I have this habit of giving kids up. I was wrong."

"Lizzie," Pop said.

She said, "But we love him too much. We have to keep him with us. We have to fight for him. We have to *fight* for him."

"That's different than telling me 'You fight for him.' I want to be sure about this, Lizzie."

"Don't you question me like a suspect. And your son is sitting right there."

"I want to be sure. You're saying *we*."

"Yes."

"You are," Pop said.

Miz Bean said, "Yes." Then she said, "But he's just sitting there."

Mr. O'Nolan said, "I'm embarrassed for you both. Though inspirited." He said, "Peter? Did you hear?"

Petey heard them talking. He heard Miz Bean telling Pop how long he'd been sitting there. He thought of his fort on his trail. He thought of him and Pop standing down there and looking at everything. He knew Mom wouldn't be able to walk all the way down there and all the way back in her high heels. She'd be dressed in high heels. He felt his mouth smile. He wasn't laughing at his mother. She'd look nice. After a while they would have to go up the trail and help her.

Pop said, "Petey?"

Mr. O'Nolan said, "Perhaps you might make it clear to him that you and Lizzie intend to insist that he remain with you. Would that—Lizzie, would that reinforce his desire to, to what? Good heavens, to surface? Peter!" Mr. O'Nolan said, "Won't you come *back?*"

Pop said, "It was self-defense. The guy was aiming a rifle at us and you saved our lives, Petey. You're a hero. *Damn!* It was self-defense."

Miz Bean shouted, "You're such a goddamned detective, aren't you? You find things, don't you? Find *him.*" Miz Bean kept shouting it at Pop. "*Find* him."

He and Pop were at the fort at the end of his trail where their land ended. They were talking about the people who were waiting at the house. They were trying to decide if they'd go back.